S0-AIG-227

Mystery at Kittiwake Bay

by Joyce A. Stengel

SCHOLASTIC INC.

New York Toronto London Auckland Sydney
Mexico City New Delhi Hong Kong Buenos Aires

No part of this publication may be reproduced in whole or in part, or stored in a retrieval system, or transmitted in any form or by any means, electronic, mechanical, photocopying, recording, or otherwise, without written permission of the publisher. For information regarding permission, write to Aladdin Paperbacks, Simon & Schuster Children's Publishing Division, 1230 Avenue of the Americas, New York, NY 10020.

ISBN 0-439-54449-1

12 11 10 9 8 7 6 5 4 3 2 1   3 4 5 6 7 8/0

Printed in the U.S.A.   40

First Scholastic printing, March 2003

Designed by Debra Sfetsios
The text of this book was set in Garamond Three

In loving memory of my mother,

Alice M. Slocum

Chapter One

Cassie Hartt propped her bike against a tree in front of the Kittiwake Grocery and lifted her long red hair from her damp neck. Drawn by a glimmer of light far out in the ocean, she crossed Sail Street to Waterview Way. At the very tip of the fingerlike cliff, Cassie made out the shape of a huge house. Light glowed in a few windows, and in the darkening, cloud-shrouded sky the house looked ghostly. The unfamiliar roar of the Atlantic pounding the eastern base of the cliff rumbled in Cassie's ears. Goose bumps crept over her skin, and she shivered.

"Come on, Sam," Cassie called to her big collie, who was busy poking his long snout into rock fissures and scrubby bushes. Sam barked and darted from the bluff down the steep street toward the quiet bay to the west. He frolicked along the beach, then froze like a pointer. Growling, he nosed at something in the sand.

Cassie, breathing hard, caught up to him. There, in a tide pool, lay a panting fish. Cassie knelt in the damp sand and looked down on the fish in his small prison, his silver stomach going up and down like a mechanical toy.

"Oh, poor thing, you can't breathe," she murmured, her throat closing with remembered panic. "I've got to get you out of there and back into the sea."

Sam barked, and moved to stand protectively in front of Cassie, growling low in his throat. Cassie's heart lurched when she saw the shadowy form approaching them.

"Hey, does he bite?" called a boy.

"Quiet, Sam," Cassie commanded, studying the boy, who brushed a lock of sandy hair from his forehead. He doesn't look dangerous, she thought. "Not unless I want him to," she said.

"Uh, do you want him to?"

Cassie laughed. "No, I guess not."

"What's so interesting in the sand?"

"A stranded fish. Look at him. He'll suffocate if we don't get him back in the water."

They gazed down on the fish, motionless except

for his silver body heaving up and down. "I saw a kid's pail back there. I'll get it," said the boy, loping off. Cassie watched him search for the pail, then fill it with seawater. Nice, she thought. Maybe a little older than me? Fourteen or fifteen? And just about my height.

"Here's the water of salvation," said the boy, setting the pail down. "Do you want to do the honors or do you want me to?"

"I will," said Cassie. "I know just how he feels." She seized the slippery body, but the fish thrashed and nearly slid from her hands. Her throat swelling with fear, she grasped him and thrust him into the pail. Sam, barking wildly, circled Cassie and the boy as they made their way to the sea's edge. Cassie tipped the bucket and, in a shimmering flash, the fish swam to freedom. Cassie breathed a sigh of relief, then laughing, turned and hastened across the beach toward the road, Sam at her heels.

"What did you mean you knew just how the fish felt?" asked the boy, jogging beside her.

Cassie slowed to a walk. "Oh, it's just that years ago, when I was four or five . . . I was at a birthday party . . . and we were playing hide-and-seek in the basement. I hid in a closet filled with clothes. Somehow the door got locked, and everyone went upstairs for cake and ice cream . . . and forgot all about me." Cassie ran her fingers over her throat, remembering the choking odor of mothballs, the feel of rough fabric against her face. "Anyway, ever since then, I've hated small spaces."

"Claustrophobia," said the boy.

"What?" said Cassie.

"You have claustrophobia—a fear of confining spaces."

"That's me, all right."

"You're new here," said the boy.

"Just moved in today." Cassie's thoughts swerved from the silver fish and the boy to why she was here in Kittiwake Bay, Maine, far from Bakersville, Ohio, where she had lived since she was born. The reality of her parents' divorce and her father's plans to remarry crashed down on her, crushing the excitement of rescuing the fish and meeting a cute guy.

They topped the hill and stood in front of the Kittiwake Grocery. "I've got to get some food before the store closes," said Cassie. "My mother and brother will think I've gotten lost."

"I'm Marc. Marc Nolan. What's your name?"

"Cassie Hartt."

"Hi, Cassie Hartt. I'm probably late, too," said Marc. "See you around." He sprinted across the street and up the rise to Waterview Way. Cassie, climbing the wooden steps to the store, wondered if he lived in that spooky house.

A short time later, she left the grocery with bags of sandwich makings, milk, juice, and cereal. She secured them in the basket and, grasping the handlebars, wheeled the bike away from the tree, then stopped and booted down the kickstand. "Come on, Sam, one more look," she murmured.

She climbed the hill across the street and peered down the cliff road. Thick clouds hid the new moon. She could no longer see the house, just its yellow lights, eerie in the dark night. It was quiet except for the urgent splash of water far below.

As Cassie gazed at the house, a bright light, higher in the darkness than the other lights, flashed three times, stopped, then again flashed three times.

Barking sharply, Sam ran to the bay side of the cliff.

"Come on, Sam. We've got to get home," Cassie called.

Sam, growling, stood his ground.

"Come on, Sam," Cassie insisted, catching him by the collar. "Quiet down. You'll wake the dead."

Clouds shifted, and in the momentary moon-light, Cassie saw two figures dart back among the rocks. The sound of muffled angry voices drifted up to her.

Cassie's heart pounded. "Come, Sam," she whispered, tugging at his collar and stepping back from her vantage point, worried that the stealthy figures had seen her.

Cassie jumped on her bike and raced past the grocery store to Shore Road. What were those people doing on the cliff at night? she wondered. What was that flashing light all about?

The roar of the sea battering the high bluff along Shore Road boomed in Cassie's ears. Her pulse thundering, she pedaled down the sloping way, flying past the bluff, shadowy dunes, and dark, ever-moving surf. To her left, woods rose high above her; trees swayed and moaned in the wind.

Relieved to leave the desolate road, Cassie wheeled the bike left onto Omega Street. Two streets down she turned left again onto Fairway Drive and biked past the main house of Fairway Estate, which stood far back on the right side of the road. Finally, she crossed Fairway Drive where it curved west to the estate's three-car garage, and coasted to the back steps of the guest house her mother had rented.

She hopped off the bike and knelt down to

wait for Sam. The big dog lumbered to her and she hugged him, murmuring against his heaving side, "I'm sorry, old boy. I shouldn't have made you run so hard. But those flashing lights, then the voices . . . they really spooked me." Sam nuzzled her ear and gave her a wet kiss.

"That you, Cassie?" her mother called from the kitchen.

Cassie hoisted the groceries and hurried into the well-lit kitchen. In the bright room, with her mother unpacking dishes, she felt foolish. What had she been fleeing? Nothing but her own silly fear.

"I was a little worried," said her mother. "After you left, Ellen Fairway stopped over. She was saying there've been a lot of robberies lately."

Chapter Two

Cassie shoved a box of books toward the bookcase in her new room. It was early Sunday afternoon, and all morning they'd been unpacking. Yesterday, she'd helped her mother set up the kitchen. She'd lined the cabinets with shelf paper, washed and dried the dishes, and tried to get seven-year-old Danny to help while their mother went grocery-shopping.

Now, finally, she had a chance to fix up the room that was going to be hers. First, she organized her clothes, then started on the books.

"Cassie?" Her mother rapped on the door and came in. She sat on the bed and ran her hands through her short, reddish-brown hair. Cassie noticed the dark circles under her hazel eyes. People said they looked alike. Cassie knew they had the same coloring, but her mother was tall and graceful while Cassie felt that she was all arms and legs that got in her way.

"Cassie, honey, please take Danny to the beach. He's driving me crazy! I can't get anything accomplished," her mother pleaded.

"But, Mom, I wanted to sort out this stuff."

"I know, honey, but you can work on it later. You know, Cassie, I'm depending on you to keep an eye on Danny this summer."

Cassie nodded. Her mother was a nurse and started work tomorrow at City Hospital, a good thirty miles away. Since she'd be traveling so far and working different shifts, Cassie would be responsible for Danny.

"Why don't you walk down with us, Mom? You look tired."

"Not today. I'll feel better if I can just get things pulled together."

Danny skipped ahead of Cassie down Omega Street to Shore Road.

"Hurry up, Cassie. I want to see the beach."

Cassie glanced at the overcast sky. Its gloominess made her think of the great house looming over the ocean. She was anxious to see it close up, to explore it. Maybe tomorrow. But she'd have to take Danny.

"Come on, Sam. Come on," shouted Danny,

dancing around the dog and exciting him to a frenzy of barking. "We're going to the beach. We're going to the beach," he chanted.

Cassie smiled. It was good to see Danny happy. Since their father had moved out, he'd been unpredictable, sometimes loud and obnoxious, sometimes sullen and withdrawn. Now, his red hair blazed in a shaft of sun that broke through the clouds, and he seemed more his old self.

Cassie, six years older than Danny, had always mothered him a little. But now she'd be responsible for him. How could she meet people? How could she do anything interesting? It was only late June. School didn't start until September. A lonely, boring summer stretched ahead of her.

They skidded down a steep path to the rock-strewn beach. Sam, sliding down behind them, showered them with sand and stones. Danny tore ahead to the water's edge, his sneakers marking his trail in the damp sand. Sam raced beside him, barking and scattering sandpipers that dashed about on pipestem legs.

Cassie pulled a Frisbee from her beach bag. "Danny, catch," she called, flinging it through the air. Danny raced after the blue disk, but Sam was quicker. He snatched it in his mouth and galloped back to Cassie.

"So you want to play, too," said Cassie, laughing and tossing the disk to Danny. Danny ran to catch it with Sam at his heels. Overhead, seagulls reeled and called.

Danny, tearing toward the massive cliffs that towered in the distance, suddenly turned back, wide-eyed and pointing. "Cassie, there's a whole bunch of kids up there, and look. There's a girl with a cat on a leash! I want a cat. Do you think I could get a kitten, Cassie? You've got Sam."

Cassie stared. Sure enough, down the beach came a girl with a cat on a leash. Sam trotted off to investigate. Cassie burst out laughing when the cat arched its back and hissed, scaring Sam, who scooted back.

The girl let the leash go and quickly pulled a camera from the pocket of her oversized blue shirt and snapped a picture of the cat and dog.

"Sam! Come, Sam," called Cassie, running toward them. "He won't hurt your cat."

"Hope I got that picture," the girl said, scrambling for the leash.

Up close, Cassie could see that the girl was older than she had first thought. She was tiny, about five feet tall and slender. The wind tousled the short dark curls framing her heart-shaped face. What Cassie had thought was a long earring was a tiny

11

braid swinging in front of her left ear. Braces glinted in her mouth. She stooped and picked up the bristly cat. "Quiet, Minerva. Quiet," she soothed.

"I'm sorry if Sam scared your cat," said Cassie.

"She's all right now," said the girl.

"Can I hold her?" breathed Danny.

"Sure," said the girl, holding the cat out to Danny, who clutched the squirming animal to his chest.

"Who are all those kids?" he asked, nodding his head toward the cliff.

The girl turned and squinted back at the group of young children. "That's the Beachcombers Club. It's for kids six through ten. They go swimming, camping, stuff like that. They meet in an old cottage over on Sail Street every morning."

Cassie listened intently. A club for kids Danny's age. "That sounds like fun, doesn't it, Danny? Maybe you'd like to join that club," she said.

"Maybe," Danny mumbled, intent on stroking the cat.

"I'm Liz Painter," said the girl, turning to Cassie. "You're living in the Fairways' guest house, right? I live on Pepperidge Lane, right on the other side of the hedge. We're neighbors." Liz smiled, covering her mouth with her hand.

Probably to hide her braces, Cassie thought.

"I'm Cassie Hartt, and this is my brother, Danny."

"You here for the summer?" asked Liz.

"No, for good, I guess," said Cassie.

"You mean you'll be going to school here in the fall?" Liz asked.

Cassie nodded. "How old are you?"

"Thirteen."

"Me, too. We'll be in the same class!" Liz said, her voice rising to a squeal. They walked down the beach, then turned toward the steep path that led to the road.

"I'll walk with you," said Liz. "I'm on my way to the Fairways' to baby-sit." They started up Omega Street, Liz chattering away, Danny walking the cat on its leash, and Sam trotting behind them.

"How about coming to the Sand Shack with me tonight? Maybe some of the kids will be there. Some of the boys," said Liz, giggling.

"Sounds great," said Cassie, hoping her mother would say yes, praying she wouldn't have to baby-sit Danny.

Chapter Three

A warm ocean breeze carried the salty smell of the sea to Cassie as she biked up Shore Road with Liz. They turned onto Sail Street and started past the Kittiwake Grocery. In front of the store, Cassie squeezed her handbrakes and, straddling her bike, gazed at the house sitting high on the cliff's outermost point. A few lights shone dimly in the dusky sky.

"Cassie, hurry up," called Liz, waiting in front of the tackle and fishing store.

Cassie was tempted to tell Liz about the flashing lights she had seen Friday night. But something held her back. She decided to wait and investigate on her own.

"Come on," Liz urged. "The Sand Shack is just up the street."

In the wood-paneled coffee shop, ceiling fans whirled soundlessly and overhead lights cast a dim glow. Cassie and Liz sat in a wooden booth where windows overlooked the bay.

"We can see if anybody interesting comes," said Liz.

Cassie gazed out the window. In the misty light, the land across the bay was a murky strip separating light gray sky from dark gray sea. Lights on a few boats bobbed on the water.

It was bright and cheerful in the old-fashioned restaurant. An ancient cash register clanged every time the waitress opened and shut it. A red-bordered rectangular tray picturing a blond girl raising a Coca-Cola bottle to her lips, and an orange tin tray advertising Orange Crush for five cents added color to the walls. Two glass-covered cake dishes stood on the counter, one holding a chocolate cake and the other a pie.

Liz, tense with excitement, grabbed Cassie's arm. "They're coming. Don't turn around. But they're coming. I thought Ryan was working tonight, but they're both here. Wait till you see them. Don't turn around, though. They're both scrumptious, but especially Ryan." Liz's hand covered her braces, smothering her giggles.

Cassie heard the screen door squeak open, then

15

slam shut. The edge of the wooden seat pressed into her bare legs. She was dying to look at the boys but didn't dare turn her head.

"Hey, Liz. How's it going?" asked a dark-haired boy sliding in to the booth next to Liz.

Liz is right, thought Cassie. He is scrumptious. The boy had dark brown eyes and jet-black hair. His tight, sleeveless jersey clung to his muscular chest.

"Cassie, this is Ryan Jerrick," said Liz, gazing up at him. "And Marc Nolan," she said as Marc slid next to Cassie.

Cassie's legs stuck to the wooden bench and made it hard to slide over. She flushed, hoping she didn't look too awkward. She turned her head to look at Marc and noticed that his eyes were a deep, clear blue.

He smiled. "Any fish tonight?"

Cassie grinned. "Not that I know of."

"What are you talking about?" asked Ryan.

As Marc was telling them about the fish, the waitress cut in. "What will you kids have?" she asked.

After they ordered sundaes, Liz said, "Cassie just moved here from the Midwest."

"The Midwest? You didn't have any ocean there," said Ryan.

Cassie looked at him as she answered, but his dark gaze never quite focused on her. "No, it's so different here. I'd never seen the ocean before."

"Never seen the ocean? I can't imagine not living near water," said Marc, shaking his head.

"Marc is crazy about boats," said Liz.

"Someday," Marc said, "I'll have enough money to buy one."

Ryan looked out at the somber bay. "If you like water, Cassie, you're in the right town. This place is surrounded by it."

"Especially the cliff with that big house on it," said Cassie, a little shiver passing through her as she thought of the house looming against the dark sky.

"When were you there?" Ryan asked in a sharp voice.

"That's Waterview Manor," said Marc. "It's a senior citizens' residence where Ryan and I work. We just came from there, actually. I used to volunteer, but now that I'm fifteen, I get cold cash."

Ryan spooned a dripping mound of hot fudge and chocolate ice cream into his mouth. "Senior citizens' residence," he muttered. "It's more like a deserted mausoleum. And the people are a bunch of mummies—ancient, and half dead."

"It wasn't always a seniors' residence," said Liz.

17

"There're all kinds of stories about the place. I bet it's haunted. It sure looks it, especially at night."

Marc chuckled. "It is pretty old, but I haven't seen any ghosts." Turning toward Cassie, he said, "It's an interesting place. It was built before the Civil War by some rich guy. In the fifties it was deeded to the town, then just stood there empty while the town decided what to do with it. Finally, they decided to close off one wing and turn the rest into an old people's home."

"That's when they fixed the place up a little," Ryan added.

Marc scraped the metal ice-cream dish with his spoon. "The people living there love it. It's got such great views."

"Didn't you tell me it was once part of the Underground Railroad, Ryan?" Liz asked, fiddling with her tiny braid.

"According to know-it-all Mrs. Wentworth," Ryan said.

Marc shot Ryan an annoyed look. "Well, she's lived here in Kittiwake all her life, and she must be eighty-five or more."

"We studied the Underground Railroad last year," Cassie said. "It was wonderful how so many people helped the slaves escape from the South."

"Mrs. Wentworth says her grandfather helped," Marc said.

Liz finished her ice cream and wiped her mouth with a napkin. "I wonder why they called it the Underground Railroad. It wasn't really underground and it wasn't a railroad."

"The slave owners started calling it that when they couldn't find their runaway slaves. They said it was like they had just disappeared on an underground railroad," Cassie explained.

"Mrs. Wentworth is really proud of Kittiwake's role in helping those runaways," Marc said. "And her other big story is Captain Kidd's treasure. Ryan and I have heard it a million times."

"Not much chance of it being here in Kittiwake, Maine," Ryan muttered. "I bet every town along the coast thinks it has Captain Kidd's treasure. Mrs. Wentworth's an old windbag. Not worth listening to."

Cassie blurted, "You don't seem to like the people very much, Ryan. Why do you work there?"

Ryan's dark eyes flashed. "I work because I need the money," he snapped.

An awkward silence settled over the group. There I go again, speaking before thinking, thought Cassie.

Liz giggled nervously. "Maybe there really is treasure out there."

"Maybe I could volunteer at Waterview Manor, like you used to, Marc," said Cassie, thinking it would give her the opportunity to explore the mysterious house and fill the long summer days. That is, if Danny joined the Beachcombers.

Marc nodded. "It's fun," he said. "The residents are lonely and like company. Some of them never get any visitors."

"They may not need any more help, though," said Ryan.

Marc shrugged off Ryan's objection and said to Cassie, "I start helping out at the yacht club next week, so I'll only be able to work at Waterview in the evenings. They could probably use you during the day."

The screen door behind Cassie and Marc screeched open.

"Look who's here. Ape-man himself," Ryan muttered.

"Hey, John. How's it going?" called Marc.

Cassie looked at the boy who turned toward them. Heavy-lidded eyes set in a beefy face, thick lips, mouth open slightly. About the same height as Marc and Ryan, but heavier. His long arms hung loosely at his sides.

"You working tonight, John?" asked Marc.

"On my way there now. Just thought I'd get an ice cream first." His hooded eyes lingered on Cassie.

"This is Cassie Hartt. Cassie, John Hudson. He works at Waterview, too."

"Hi, John." Cassie smiled but felt uneasy under John's unwavering stare.

"He gives me the creeps," Liz whispered when John left the Sand Shack, slurping an ice-cream cone.

"He's all right. Maybe a little dense. Strong, though. He can lift anything," said Marc.

"Liz is right. He's a creep," said Ryan. "He dropped out of high school a few years ago and has been doing odd jobs around town ever since."

"I think he liked you, Cassie," said Liz. "He couldn't take his eyes off you."

"Must be the red hair," said Marc, gently pulling Cassie's ponytail.

Cassie felt her cheeks burn. "Tell me about the hidden treasure," she pleaded, changing the subject.

"I don't know about hidden treasure," said Marc, "but someone's sure piling up treasure somewhere. There's been a ton of robberies in town. The paper says the crook or crooks seem to know just which houses to rob—who has the money."

"It's probably one of the summer people," said Ryan, scraping the last bit of chocolate from his silver dish.

"Could be," said Marc. "But most of them have been coming here for years."

"I hope they find the crooks soon," said Liz.

"You'd better be sure to lock the doors when you baby-sit at the Fairways'," warned Marc. "They're a likely target."

They separated outside the Sand Shack, Ryan and Marc turning up Sail Street. A brisk breeze blew off the water, bringing with it the salty tang of the sea. Above, a smattering of stars glittered through torn clouds.

"Aren't they scrumptious?" said Liz, sighing. "Especially Ryan. I hope he asks me out. He calls sometimes, but he hasn't asked me on a real date yet."

Ryan was handsome, Cassie mused, riding her bike in silence. But Marc had such a nice smile. She remembered his pulling her ponytail, and she felt the warm flush rising up her neck to her face. It was different somehow, different from when she was younger and pesty boys had yanked on her hair.

At the corner of Sail Street and Shore Road, Cassie crossed the street and stared at Waterview

Manor. Its lights glowed high up in the dark sky. But tonight no light flashed. She wondered why she didn't want to tell the others about the flashing light.

"Are you really thinking of volunteering there?" asked Liz, wheeling her bike next to Cassie. "It's so spooky. You wouldn't catch me there."

A shiver of fear and excitement passed through Cassie. She felt both afraid of and drawn to that great house towering above the Atlantic. "Yes," she murmured, more to herself than to Liz. "I am going to volunteer there."

Chapter Four

Cassie, half asleep, pulled her covers around her. The blanket slid away, and Sam's cold nose nuzzled her arm. Cassie reached for the blanket again, but this time her hand found Sam's silky head. "Oh, Sam, it's too early. Go back to sleep," she grumbled, curling up under the covers.

Sam grabbed the sheet and blanket in his mouth and pulled them to the floor. Cassie felt the cool morning breeze that rustled the shades at her window.

"Sam," she mumbled into the pillow. "Go away." Waking up gradually, she sat up and leaned back against her plump pillows. Her eyes fell to an unpacked carton. Once I get all my things set up, maybe this room will seem more like my own, she thought.

On either side of the window facing east, bookcases held a jumble of books and stuffed animals. One of them was a fluffy dog that resembled Sam, a birthday present when she'd turned five.

Her gaze drifted to the north wall, where two windows overlooked the Fairways' house. On the bureau between the two windows stood pictures of friends left behind in Ohio and one of her, her mother and father, and Danny. Cassie sighed. Why did everything have to change? How could this place ever be home?

Her thoughts shifted to last night, and a thrill of excitement shot through her. Ryan and Marc. Robberies in town. Treasure at the old mansion. Her thoughts kept returning to Marc. Ryan hadn't been very friendly, but he was certainly good-looking. But Marc—she felt comfortable talking to him. And Liz, she liked Liz.

"Woof. Woof." Sam's low bark brought her attention back to him.

"All right. All right. I'll take you out. I wish you'd learn to sleep late once in a while," Cassie said, swinging her long legs out of bed and reaching for her robe.

Sam followed her downstairs, his nails clicking on the wooden floor. Cassie opened the back door, and Sam bounded out toward the woods. The eastern sky was rosy pink and gold, and dew glistened on the stubby grass.

Cassie drew in a deep breath of pine-scented air, then caught sight of early summer flowers growing by the garage. Impulsively, she walked through the moist grass, blades of it slipping between her toes. She picked some wine-colored poppy mallows and daisylike golden marguerites to put on the breakfast table. Maybe they'd cheer her mother up

I know it's hard for Mom, she thought. Starting all over again. She always looks tired now.

Sam sniffed along the edge of the woods bordering the back of the property. Then, barking sharply, he disappeared into the underbrush.

"Sam," Cassie called.

But Sam continued to bark. Just like he did that night at the rocks, Cassie thought. She laid the flowers on the ground, ducked under a low-hanging branch, and picked her way carefully down a path. She could hear Sam far ahead. When she reached the spruce trees, the going was easier because the ground was padded with pine needles. Intertwining branches overhead blocked the sun and killed off everything in the shade underneath.

Cassie shivered in the cool dimness. She stood still for a moment, listening for sounds of Sam. A chill snaked down her spine, and she pulled her robe tighter. She had an eerie feeling that someone was watching her.

"Come, Sam! Come," she called, shaking herself and starting back down the path. I'm letting my imagination run away with me, she thought. Still, I'd better get back.

Sam came loping through the trees. He turned to bark once or twice, then trotted back to Cassie. As she started back down the path, she stepped on something wet and gooey. She screeched and drew her foot back, thinking she'd stepped on a small animal. But a sticky mass, partially covered with pine needles, stuck to the sole of her foot.

"Gross—gum," she mumbled in disgust. She picked up a twig and scraped her foot clean, then stared at the mass, a puzzled frown on her face.

This gum hasn't been here long, she thought. Remembering the talk about the robberies in town, Cassie's stomach knotted in fear. Someone could hide in these woods and steal into her yard or the Fairways' at night. She could hear Marc warning Liz: "You'd better be sure to lock the doors when you baby-sit at the Fairways'. They're a likely target."

Cassie headed back to the house and stopped to look through the kitchen door. Her mother sat, elbows on table, face in hands, staring at a steaming cup of black coffee.

"Morning, Mom," said Cassie, letting the door slam behind her and Sam. Holding out the purple and yellow flowers, she said, "Aren't these pretty?"

"Lovely, Cass," she said, giving them a quick glance. Disappointed, Cassie sighed and hunted for a vase to put them in. Unable to find one, she settled for a glass, arranged the flowers, and set them on the table. Then she poured herself a cup of coffee, added milk and three teaspoons of sugar, and sat down opposite her mother.

"Do you think you'll like working at City Hospital, Mom?" she asked, trying to get her mother's attention from wherever it had wandered off to.

"Um?" Her mother focused on her. "I hope so, Cassie. It will be a challenge going back to work full-time." Then, more like her old self, she smiled and asked, "Did you and Liz have a good time at the Sand Shack?"

"It's a neat place. Good ice cream. And I met two of her friends, Marc Nolan and Ryan Jerrick."

"Is Liz coming over today?"

"No, she's taking care of Christopher Fairway. She baby-sits there."

"I talked to the Beachcombers' teacher, Mrs. Antonelli, last night. She sounds very nice. I told her a little bit about Danny and that I'd be in soon to meet her. Ellen Fairway recommends the program. Says her nephew goes there and loves it. Just be sure Danny wants to stay. And be sure you get there to pick him up on time. I don't want him to feel deserted."

Cassie sighed. "I'll be on time," she promised.

Mrs. Hartt refilled her coffee cup. "And you, Cassie? What are you going to do with yourself?"

"I thought I'd see about volunteering at Waterview Manor. It's that mansion way out on the cliff. It's actually a senior citizens' residence."

Mrs. Hartt smiled. "I used to volunteer at a children's hospital when I was a teen. But I was a bit older than you."

"Marc and Ryan work there. Marc said he's been volunteering since he was twelve, reading to the people, helping them write letters."

Jean Hartt glanced at the clock. "I'll have to hear more about it later. You can check it out today, then we'll talk about it. I've got to take a shower and get ready for work. Where's that new shampoo you bought, Cassie?"

"It's in the shower rack, Mom. Just where y⟨…⟩ told me to put it."

"Okay." Jean Hartt started up the stairs, then called back, "Be sure Danny wants to stay at that club. It does sound like a good program. I just hope he agrees."

"He'd better," Cassie murmured, clearing the table.

Chapter Five

Cassie's bike rattled as she pedaled up the narrow gravel road to Waterview Manor. At times, as she crested a dip in the road or turned a curve, she could see the house sprawling at the end of the long spit of land. To her left, the land, thick with balsam fir and white spruce, sloped upward, then fell steeply to the rocky coastline of the pounding ocean far below. The trees closer to the ocean were low-growing and scraggly; shallow-rooted, they clung to rocks and leaned out over the water. Rain-laden clouds had moved in and hung low in the sky. The day had turned hot and humid. Sam loped alongside the bike, his tongue hanging out.

Cassie leaned over the handlebars, her ponytail swinging forward. She glanced to the bay side, remembering the figures she had seen there the other night. She felt a tightness in her chest, and a chill of fear shot through her. I'm being silly, she thought. This is just an old mansion. Still, she couldn't shake a premonition of danger.

Cassie dropped her bike to the ground and stood looking up at the nineteenth-century mansion built into the slope of the cliff. Two wings, jutting out from either side of the center section, rose three stories high. The center section rose four stories. From its slanted roof, an octagonal tower offered views in all directions. That must be where I saw the flashing light, thought Cassie. A covered porch ran along the front of the whole house, its straight lines curving into semicircles on either end. The east wing nestled in the shelf of the cliff. The west wing opened on grounds covered with windswept brush and wildflowers that ended abruptly at the bay-side cliff. Telling Sam to "stay," Cassie walked up the wooden steps of the veranda. A single raindrop splashed onto her forehead.

The screen door creaked as it closed behind her. She stood in the great center hall, dark and musty despite tall windows. It was filled with overstuffed chairs, and tables covered with magazines. No one was in the room. On either side, archways led to door-lined corridors. Cassie walked to the back, where a wider archway led into an empty dining room. To her right, another arched door opened into a large game room that opened into the semi-circular side porch overlooking the bay. At the back of the dining room, screened doors opened onto the porch overlooking the ocean. Through these doors came the sound of a high-pitched angry voice. Cassie hesitated, then headed toward the voice.

Cassie stepped out onto the porch and smiled at what she saw. A frail old woman confined to a wheelchair was berating Ryan Jerrick.

"Don't you sneer at me, young man. I know what I know, and I tell you . . . ," the woman scolded, her birdlike hand fingering a lavaliere that hung low on her chest. She broke off mid-sentence when Cassie appeared. "Well, who are you, miss? I don't recall seeing you before."

Ryan frowned, and Cassie thought he wasn't going to introduce her. Then, grudgingly, he said, "This is Cassie Hartt, Mrs. Wentworth."

"Hello, Mrs. Wentworth," Cassie said, smiling. "What a beautiful necklace."

Mrs. Wentworth's lined face beamed. "Thank you, dear. Come take a closer look," she said, holding the piece out on the palm of her hand.

Cassie bent over and admired two finely

wrought dark-gold rose blossoms, one dangling below the other, linked by lighter gold leaves. A diamond flashed in the center of each. "It's exquisite," she breathed.

Ryan, with a smirk in his voice, said, "Mrs. Wentworth has just been telling me the history of Kittiwake Bay." Lowering his voice slightly, he added, "Again."

"I don't like your tone, Ryan," Mrs. Wentworth said, grasping the arms of her wheelchair. "I was born in this town, and I know everything there is to know about it. Now find that Strauss tape for me, the one with the polkas."

Ryan's already high color increased. He glanced at Cassie, then walked into the dining room to a small table holding a radio and a tape player. He squatted and shuffled through a box on the shelf beneath the table.

"Maddening," Mrs. Wentworth snapped. "The way these hands and feet don't do what I want them to anymore."

Ryan stepped back onto the porch and handed her a tape. "Is this the one you want?"

Mrs. Wentworth took the tape and peered at the title. "This is it. Just slide it in and turn it on."

Ryan stalked away, slipped the tape in the tape deck, and pushed a button.

The strains of a Strauss polka filled the air, and Mrs. Wentworth started tapping her foot to the rhythm. "Ah, how Hobart and I used to polka. We were the best dancers in town. Won all sorts of prizes," she murmured, a faraway look in her eyes. Then, head tilted, she looked up at Cassie. "Now, tell me, why are you here? To visit Ryan? Is he your young man?"

"N-no," Cassie stammered, her face flaming. "I've come to see about volunteering here."

"That would be nice," said Mrs. Wentworth, a smile lighting her lined face. "It would be pleasant to have a young lady around. And, if you're interested, I can tell you all about Kittiwake Bay. Why don't you show Cassie around now, Ryan? I'll just sit here and listen to the music." She waved them away with an imperious gesture of her left arm, and Cassie smelled the delicate scent of lavender water.

Ryan was quiet a moment as he and Cassie walked down the porch, then he said, "Don't pay any attention to the stories that old windbag tells. She's a little gone up here." He tapped his head. Cassie looked into his dark eyes. Ryan might look "scrumptious," as Liz had said, but he acted arrogant. Mrs. Wentworth didn't seem confused to her.

"Do you think you really want to work here?"

Ryan asked, gesturing to the old people sitting in rockers. "It's, 'Get this. Get that.' These wrinklies keep you hopping."

"I think I'd like it, Ryan," said Cassie, looking at two white-haired gentlemen playing checkers, one chuckling triumphantly as he jumped three of his opponent's men.

Ryan introduced Mr. O'Reilly, the winner of the game, and Mr. Johnson to Cassie. When Mr. Johnson smiled, his chins quivered. Mr. O'Reilly's sparse wisps of hair fluttered in the breeze that blew in from the bay, and his teeth slipped when he spoke. "Forgot to put in the cement," he explained.

A sharp bark caught everyone's attention, and Sam nosed the screen door open and walked onto the porch. He stopped by Cassie, looked up at her, and barked again.

"Heh, heh. That your dog, lass?" asked Mr. O'Reilly.

Cassie grasped Sam's collar. "Sam, did you get tired of waiting for me? Out you go."

"No. No. Let him stay. He's all right. Here, boy. Come here, boy," said Mr. O'Reilly, reaching toward the dog. "Sam? Is that what you call him?" he asked, his veined hand gently stroking Sam's sleek head.

36

"That's his name. Short for Samson," Cassie explained.

Mr. O'Reilly nodded. "Sam. That's a right good name for a dog. Short and simple."

Ryan rocked back on his heels and slapped his hands together. "Well, Cassie, if you're sure you want to work here, I'll show you where Mrs. Sutton's office is. She's the one to talk to."

"I'm sure," said Cassie, watching the two men fuss over Sam, who seemed to be relishing the attention.

Ryan led her to the main entrance and pointed to the east corridor. "Down that hallway."

"I thought that was the closed section of the house," said Cassie.

"Most of it is. See you around. I'm off now."

Cassie stood in the entrance hall, surprised at Ryan's abrupt departure. Looking through the door, she saw him pass John Hudson on the veranda steps. They barely nodded to each other. Cassie hurried to the east corridor. She'd just as soon avoid talking to John if she could.

Mrs. Sutton, the personnel administrator, welcomed her. They could certainly use a volunteer. Cassie could spend time with the residents, playing games with them, reading to them, and writing letters for some of them. She was to report to Mrs. Sawyer, the nurse, tomorrow.

Cassie, excited at the prospect of being part of Waterview Manor, stepped from the brightness of the office into the dim hallway. To her right was the center hall. To her left, the corridor snaked off into the unused wing. Without hesitation, she turned left. Remembering the talk of ghosts and treasure, she couldn't resist the temptation to explore. She didn't really believe in ghosts, and treasure—well, you could never tell. Either way, a place as big and as old as this mansion was intriguing. Then, too, there was the flashing light she had seen.

Faint light, filtering through the transoms above the high wooden doors, showed rusting pipes running along the edge of the ceiling, dark with spidery cracks. The floor under Cassie's feet was warped and uneven. She came to a door with a sign warning NO TRESPASSING—EAST WING CLOSED. Cassie, chewing on a fingernail, squinted at the sign, then thrust the door open and slipped into the forbidden hallway.

The tomblike stillness of the maze of hallways whispered in Cassie's ears like an actual presence. Deeper and deeper she crept through the desolate labyrinth. When a mournful howl broke the silence, Cassie froze, every nerve in her body taut. Barely breathing, she waited. There it was again, a low, plaintive wailing. The sound seemed to come from behind the door at the end of a dark passage. Cassie hung back, afraid to open the door. What or who was behind it? Hand trembling, she reached forward and grabbed the knob.

She coughed and sneezed as stale, dusty air wafted into her nostrils and mouth. She found herself in a small enclosure. To her left, glass doors, crossed by nailed boards, led to the semicircular side porch. The wind rapped at the windows and sang its doleful song through spidery cracks and small holes in the glass panes.

Cassie laughed in relief. "So that's what the noise is," she murmured. "Here I am thinking I've found a ghost, and it's only the wind. Now to find my way back."

She stood in the enclosure looking at the doors that surrounded her, wondering which one to open next. Deciding on the door leading to the back of the house, she started toward it. A creaking sound stopped her. Looking over her shoulder, she saw the doorknob on the center interior door move. Her heart thudded in her chest as she watched the door swing outward. Then a dirt-smudged figure appeared.

"What are you doing here?" asked Marc Nolan, his eyebrows rising.

"I might ask you the same thing," snapped Cassie, angry at having been frightened.

"Guess I scared you, huh?" said Marc, grinning.

"I wasn't scared," Cassie asserted, annoyed. "I just didn't expect anybody. I thought this part of the house was closed off. I've been wandering around here for a while and haven't seen a soul."

"I bet you were looking for Captain Kidd's treasure," Marc said.

Cassie grinned. "No, I was just exploring. Were you looking for the treasure?"

"Sure. Why not?"

"You really believe there is one?"

"There could be. Captain Kidd was in this area. Come on, I'll show you the best way back," he said, leading her through a rear door.

Cassie followed Marc up two interior flights of steep stairs, lit only by his wavering flashlight. When they stepped out into a dank corridor, she breathed a sigh of relief, glad to leave the narrow staircase.

"This hallway snakes through the back of the house," said Marc. "But there's a more interesting way. Follow me," he said, holding his hand out like a magician toward a recessed door.

The door was loose on its hinges, and it grated like a nail against a blackboard, as Marc pulled it open, unleashing the thunderous roar of the ocean. He stepped back and shouted, "Take a look at this."

Cassie gripped the rusty iron railing of a narrow balcony and looked down. Below her, the cliff sloped from the house, then plunged to a murderous sea. Waves roared and thrashed against jutting rocks, spewing foam high into the air. Cassie stepped back and splayed her hands against the wall of the house for support. Spatters of rain splashed her face.

"Isn't it beautiful?" Marc yelled above the incessant boom of the ocean.

"It's fantastic. I've never seen anything like it. But it's kind of . . . scary. It's so . . . so powerful."

Grasping the railing and leaning forward, Marc gazed down at the pounding ocean.

"Be careful," Cassie shouted, the wind carrying her voice away. "That railing doesn't look too safe."

"I was just wondering," he said, stepping back, "exactly how this place was used to help the slaves escape. I'll have to ask Mrs. Wentworth more about it."

"Mrs. Wentworth? What about what Ryan says?"

"Oh, she's not crazy. Eccentric, maybe," Marc said, leaning toward her. "She'll tell you all her stories if you volunteer here. Are you going to?"

He pushed his hair from his forehead and smiled into her eyes.

"Yes, I am. I start tomorrow."

"Good," said Marc, so close Cassie could feel his breath on her neck.

She felt the heat rising in her face. At least Marc was glad to have her here, a nice change from Ryan.

"Come on," said Marc. "We can get to the back veranda this way. Don't worry, it's safe enough."

Cassie hoped so. She hugged the back of the old mansion as she followed him, conscious of the battering waves far below and uncertain of the swaying balcony. She wondered what stories Mrs. Wentworth could tell about the Underground Railroad. She couldn't wait to find out.

Chapter Six

It was late afternoon when Cassie left Waterview Manor. Marc had introduced her to more of the residents, and she had enjoyed talking with them. They loved Sam, and he had readily submitted to their petting.

Riding down Waterview Way, Sam running beside her, Cassie tried to sort out the impressions of the afternoon. The rambling house on the spit of land above the Atlantic Ocean promised to make the summer an exciting one. Both Ryan and Marc worked there. Marc was friendlier. And Ryan—he was handsome and mysterious, hard to understand. But Liz sure liked him.

Then there were the old people. Mrs. Wentworth and Mr. O'Reilly, the champion checkers player, were delightful. It would be like having grandparents. Her own family seemed fractured. Her father was worlds away, and her mother was busy working, trying to start a new life for herself.

And, there was the house itself. It intrigued her. It was so old and big—there must be a mystery in it. Maybe there really was a hidden treasure.

Cassie felt a splat of rain on her hand, then on her neck. She glanced at the darkening sky. A gust of wind blew wet in her face. I'd better hurry, she thought. I'm already late meeting Danny, and this is his first day. Mom will be furious.

At the end of Waterview Way, Cassie turned left onto Sail Street. The Beachcombers' cottage was farther up the street, past the center of town. Cassie pedaled by the Kittiwake Grocery, the tackle and fishing store, a general store, and the Sand Shack. On the other side of the street, boats bobbed about like toys in the unusually rough water of the bay, and seagulls cried raucously.

The road curved and climbed steeply. Cassie bent low over the handlebars of her bike to gain momentum and make herself a smaller target for the wind. Scraggly spruce trees clung to the rocky ledge that jutted over the road. On top of the ledge, evergreens towered close together. The road leveled out, and Cassie turned off to the Beachcombers' cottage and propped her bike against its side. The cottage was surrounded by dark woods, and lichen, waving and streaming in the wind, hung in long strands from the spruce. Cassie shuddered when a strand brushed her face with ghostlike tendrils.

"Oh, my dear, there you are! Danny's been waiting for you," said Mrs. Antonelli as Cassie, Sam right behind her, hurried into the cottage. She was a large, dark-haired woman with laugh lines around her brown eyes.

"You're late, Cassie . . . and Tommy called me 'Fire Head,'" complained Danny, standing hands on hips and legs wide apart.

"I'm sorry," said Cassie. "I lost track of the time. It won't happen again. I promise."

Danny, his lower lip thrust out, glared at her.

"Come on, we'd better hurry. It's starting to rain. When we get home, I'll tell you about this great old house I'm going to work in."

"You should be on time," he said. He turned and headed for the back wall where his jacket hung on a peg.

"I think Danny will fit in with the group, Cassie, but he and Tommy Cullin did quarrel and fight today. Ask your mother to give me a call. I'd like to meet her soon."

"I'll tell her," Cassie said, wishing Danny weren't such a problem.

Mrs. Antonelli peered out the window at the dark sky. "Why don't you children leave your bikes here for the night? I'll give you a ride home."

Sam nosed Cassie's hand. Cassie scratched the dog's head. "Thank you, Mrs. Antonelli, but it won't take us long to get home."

"Well, if you're sure. Better hustle though. Looks like there's going to be quite a storm."

As Cassie and Danny hurried to their bikes and coasted out from the side of the cottage, the ominous sky burst open, letting loose a downpour. Sam suddenly growled and ran toward the woods, but came back at Cassie's sharp command. Just then, wavy beams of light from a passing car lit two figures at the edge of the dark woods.

Cassie turned onto Sail Street with a vivid image etched in her mind: a short, thin man wearing a red sweatshirt talking intently to a younger man. As he talked, he emphasized his words with angry jabs of his right arm. The younger man looked furious, standing with his hands on hips, head held straight despite the rain. It was the image of the younger man that stayed with Cassie. She could have sworn that it was Ryan Jerrick.

Chapter Seven

Liz rapped on the back door, opened it, and let it slam behind her. "Cassie, I'm here."

"Up here," called Cassie.

Liz bounded up the stairs. "Wait till you see the picture I took! Remember the day I first met you on the beach? I took a picture of Minerva and Sam. Take a look," she gasped, flying into Cassie's room out of breath.

"Hey, this is really good." Cassie laughed when she looked at the shot of Sam backing away from the arch-backed Minerva. "Sam, look at what a chicken you are," she said, scooting to the floor and giving Sam a hug. He opened his eyes, thumped his tail, and went back to sleep.

Liz beamed. "My father says it's contest material."

"You're really into photography, aren't you?"

"I want to be a professional someday. Wait till you see all the pictures I've taken. And soon, I'll have my own darkroom. My father says if I save enough to pay half, he'll put in the rest and help me build one in the fall. Then I could do all kinds of photo projects."

"I like this one," said Cassie, looking at a picture of Minerva sitting with her tail curled around her, staring out a window at a bird.

"And look what I just got," said Liz, opening a camera bag and pulling out an expensive-looking camera. "It's even got extra lenses, a wide-angle and a close-up."

"Neat!" said Cassie. "Is it your birthday?"

Liz flushed scarlet and tugged on her tiny braid. "No. It's not really mine, just sort of a loan."

"You know," said Cassie, "I bet the people at Waterview Manor would love to have you take their pictures. Why don't you come up with me someday and do it?"

Liz hesitated. "I'd like to. I love old people's faces. But . . . that house . . ."

"Come on, Liz. It's only an old house, and it would be during the day," Cassie urged, not telling her how, late afternoons, coasting down Waterview Way on her bike, she felt like the house was watching her and, uneasy, she would look back over her shoulder at the tower windows, blinding in the afternoon sun.

Liz grinned. "I guess I sound like a big baby. But the place looks so spooky. Do you really like working there?"

Cassie nodded. "I love the oldsters. They have so many good stories. Especially Mrs. Wentworth. She's promised to tell me about Captain Kidd's treasure."

"Ryan says she's 'a foolish old bat.' I guess he doesn't like her."

Ryan doesn't seem to like anybody, Cassie thought, except Liz. "I think you'd like her," she said.

"I'd really like to take their pictures. I'll come," Liz said decisively. "Maybe someday next week, when Mrs. Fairway doesn't need me to baby-sit."

One morning the following week, Cassie was in Mrs. Wentworth's room preparing her for her photograph. The room overlooked the back veranda and smelled pleasantly of lavender water. Cassie pulled a silver-backed brush through Mrs. Wentworth's long, still luxuriant hair.

"You have good hands, Cassie. Quick, but gentle," said the old lady. "That Mrs. Sawyer wants me to cut my hair off. 'Have it short,' she says. 'It's easier to take care of.' But I like it long. My Hobart liked it long, too. And I can still manage to do it myself." A note of pride had crept into her voice.

"Your hair's so soft and silky. And it's so white— just like snow. It would be a shame to cut it," said Cassie, deftly winding and pinning Mrs. Wentworth's tresses into a knot on top of her head.

"Don't let Mrs. Sawyer hear you say that. She would fire you for insubordination." Mrs. Wentworth chuckled and admired her hairdo in the dresser mirror. Then her gaze fell and swept the clutter of pictures on the bureau. "There's Hobart and me on our wedding day," she said, pointing.

Cassie picked up the old-fashioned silver frame and studied the picture. Hobart Wentworth was tall and slim, with a neat little mustache. He stood stiff and straight in a three-piece suit. Mrs. Wentworth's dark hair was piled high on her head, and her lavaliere of gold roses and diamonds lay on the bosom of a white frilly bodice. "You were so beautiful," Cassie breathed.

Mrs. Wentworth laughed musical little notes. Then, touching her lavaliere, she murmured, "That was the first time I wore this, my wedding day." She settled herself in her electric wheelchair.

51

"Now, Cassie. You be a dear and get me some clean towels from the linen closet, then hop to the dining room and turn on some Strauss."

Cassie placed the picture back on the bureau. "Okay, Mrs. Wentworth. If you see Mr. O'Reilly, remind him that my friend Liz is coming this afternoon."

Mrs. Wentworth buzzed her wheelchair to the door. "I'll remind him to put his teeth in," she called over her shoulder.

On her way to the linen closet, Cassie stopped at the utility room to drop off the soiled towels. As she entered the room, John Hudson looked up from loading a dryer, his meaty face a blotchy red from the hot, moist air.

"Hi, Cassie," he mumbled, and laughed. Or was it a snigger? Cassie squirmed under his stare. Those long arms really do make him look like an ape, she thought, watching him swing wet towels into the dryer.

"Hi, John," she said in a rush, eager to get away. "Gotta get Mrs. Wentworth some clean towels."

Cassie hurried down the hall to the linen closet, glad to leave the steamy room and John Hudson. She yanked on the sticky door to open it and stepped into the small room lined with shelves stacked high with bed and bath linens.

Dust and lint tickled Cassie's nose. Anxious to leave the stuffy room, she quickly assembled a set of towels. Suddenly, the door slammed shut, and the door-controlled light died. In the immediate darkness, she heard footsteps thudding away. A choking, suffocating sensation overwhelmed her. Keep calm, she told herself, you're not a six-year-old now. She pushed on the door, but it was stuck tight. Her head throbbed, and her long red hair clung to her forehead and neck. At last, with a forceful shove, the door gave way and Cassie rushed out right into Ryan's arms.

"What's with you? You look like you just ran a mile," he said, steadying her with strong hands.

Cassie brushed her hair back from her face and lifted it off her neck. Her breath came in long gulps. "I couldn't get out of the closet," she gasped, her fingers stretching the collar of her shirt.

"You sure look like you could use a swim," he said, his hands warm on her shoulders. "Too bad you spend all your time here. You could be soaking up rays at the beach." He ran his hands down her arms before releasing her.

Cassie stepped back. "I like it here," she said defensively.

"You don't even get paid. If I didn't need the money, I could find lots better things to do."

Cassie, looking into his dark eyes, felt uneasy. "Well, I told Mrs. Wentworth I'd put some Strauss on," she said, picking up the towels she had dropped. She dashed to Mrs. Wentworth's room, left the towels there, then hurried to the ladies' room, where she held a cold, wet cloth against her face till her racing heart slowed down.

Later that afternoon, Liz arrived. After Cassie introduced her, Liz pulled out her camera and, taking a great deal of time, shot some pictures. "I'm not used to focusing this," she apologized. "Just stay like that a little bit longer."

"Feels like my face is going to freeze in this silly smile," said Mrs. Wentworth, trying not to move her mouth. Liz clicked the shutter, and Mrs. Wentworth wheeled her chair to the veranda railing. "Take another one, Liz. You'll get a nice background picture of the bay if I sit here," she ordered. "But, wait. Just a minute. Cassie, you check my hair. Is it still in place?" she asked, smoothing a few escaped tendrils.

Cassie tucked the escapees into the topknot, and Liz snapped another picture. Other residents crowded around and wanted their pictures taken. Liz shot Mr. O'Reilly and Mr. Johnson playing checkers. Mr. O'Reilly mugged it up and, at one point, thrust his false teeth out of his mouth. Liz squealed in delight. "Maybe I can enter that in a contest," she said.

"If you win, I get a cut of the prize," Mr. O'Reilly said, teasing her.

Liz glanced at her watch. "I have to get going. I'm due at the Fairways' soon and I want to get some scenic shots of the bay. Maybe I'll try a close-up lens," she said, peering into her camera bag.

After she left, with a promise to return with the pictures when they were developed, Cassie settled down for a checkers game with Mr. O'Reilly.

With a triumphant chuckle he captured her last man and said, "I beat you again, Cassie, but it was close. You're a good little player. Keep it up and one day you just might beat me."

"Thanks, Mr. O'Reilly, but I don't think I ever will. You're too good at games."

"I'll tell you the best game, the one that makes you use the old noodle," he said, tapping his head, where his few wisps of hair stood straight up. He paused a moment, then intoned, "Chess. Now there's a game."

"I've always wanted to learn to play chess," said Cassie.

"You mean you haven't seen his prized chess set? I thought he'd shown it to everyone here," said Mrs. Wentworth, guiding her chair closer to them.

"Now, Isabelle, don't start on me. You know it's a beautiful set. Worth a lot of money, too. I was very honored when I won it," said Mr. O'Reilly, straightening his thin shoulders and lifting his head proudly.

"What's it like?" asked Cassie, placing the checkers in a box.

"Every piece is carved from wood, and they fit into your hand just like they belong there. It's a beautiful set—a work of art."

"I'd love to see it," said Cassie.

"Would you, lass? Well, let me get it. It's way back in my closet. I'll get it and give you your first chess lesson. It's not everyone I'd let handle that set, but you've got the makings of a good chess player. I can tell by the way you play checkers." Mr. O'Reilly got up slowly from his chair, placed his hands on the back of his hips, and leaned back, stretching the stiffness from his muscles, then shuffled off to his room.

"I haven't seen him move so fast in ages," quipped Mrs. Wentworth. "He certainly is proud of that chess set. Maybe it is worth something, but not as much as my lavaliere." She sighed, fingering the necklace.

"It's really beautiful," Cassie said.

Mrs. Wentworth caressed the lovely piece of

jewelry. "This was my wedding gift from my Hobart. Ah, I remember the day as if it were yesterday."

"You must have a lot of good memories," said Cassie.

A pensive expression softened Mrs. Wentworth's features. "Good? Some are good, Cassie, but others aren't. . . . Then, of course, there's all the interesting things that went on in this town."

"Like what?" prompted Cassie, leaning her elbows on the card table and resting her chin in her hands. "You promised you'd tell me about Captain Kidd's treasure."

"Yes, it is a good possibility that Captain Kidd's treasure is buried out there in some cave. But my favorite story is how this old mansion was used as a station for runaway slaves."

"You mean when it was part of the Underground Railroad?" Cassie asked, eyes wide.

"Yes. Those were days of danger and excitement," said Mrs. Wentworth, gazing out across the bay. "Madison Palmer, a very wealthy man, built this mansion, with its labyrinth of rooms, in the mid-eighteen hundreds. It provided accommodations for summer boarders. He was good friends with my grandfather, who had money in his own right. They both hated slavery."

"So Mr. Palmer and your grandfather helped the Underground Railroad? It's a strange term, isn't it? It makes you think of trains going through dark tunnels."

Mrs. Wentworth's eyes sparkled. "The history of the slaves' escape route from the South is full of railroad terms. Once it became known as the Underground Railroad, the people involved started using railroad language. My grandfather was a conductor. That was the most dangerous job. He traveled into the Southern states and guided the escaped slaves from one safe house to another."

"What about Mr. Palmer? What did he do?"

"He allowed this house to be used as a shelter— or, in railroad talk, a station. And he was a stationmaster."

"And the runaways were passengers," Cassie said. "I remember that from a report I wrote in school last year."

Mrs. Wentworth nodded. "That's right. The escaped slaves were the passengers. And everyone involved was in danger. Especially the slaves. If they were caught, they were returned to their owners, or worse yet, hanged."

"I don't remember reading that Maine was involved. I thought the slaves were safe once they got this far north."

"No. The Fugitive Slave Law allowed slave owners to capture runaways no matter where they were in the United States. The slaves weren't really safe until they reached Canada, since slave catchers weren't allowed there."

A sudden brisk breeze blew a few magazines off one of the tables. Cassie picked them up and placed them under a heavy book, then sat back down. "What did they do with the runaways once they were here?"

"Hand me that throw, would you, Cassie?" Mrs. Wentworth asked, indicating a light cotton blanket draped over a chair. "No matter how hot it is, I always feel chilly in a breeze."

Cassie arranged the blanket around Mrs. Wentworth's shoulders, then pulled her chair closer. Mrs. Wentworth, looking at her expectant face, laughed. "I wish my students were as attentive when I taught history all those years ago. Well, let's see. My grandfather said there was a secret room somewhere across the bay. When it was safe, someone in the house would climb the steps to the tower and light a lantern. Then they would smuggle the runaways into the house, feed them, let them rest up, give them some money, and, when it was time, spirit them down a tunnel that leads to the ocean. Then they'd get into a boat and be off to Canada and freedom," she said, with a dramatic wave of her hand toward the north.

"You mean a tunnel that leads to the bay?" said Cassie, thinking of the turbulent waters on the ocean side.

"Now you sound like Ryan. Not believing me. That nice young man, Marc Nolan, he believes me. I always wanted my grandfather to show me the tunnel, but he wouldn't. He said it was too dangerous. Then I remember talk about them blocking the tunnel. I'm not sure when that happened."

"I just don't understand how anyone could launch a small boat in such rough water," Cassie mused.

"They did it somehow," Mrs. Wentworth insisted.

Cassie didn't want Mrs. Wentworth to know she doubted her, so she said, "And Captain Kidd's treasure—do you really think it's here?"

Mrs. Wentworth buzzed her chair around so her back was to the salt-smelling breeze. "That goes way back. Before this house was even built. Did you ever read about Captain Kidd?"

Cassie nodded. "The pirate."

"They called him a pirate. But the true story is he was really a victim of circumstance—a pawn, you might say, in a game played by King William

III and Richard Coote, the Earl of Bellomont."

"What do you mean—a victim of circumstance?"

"The story is that King William had authorized Captain Kidd to wage war against the real pirates, who were attacking merchant ships sailing from England to the colonies. But he also allowed him to prey on French merchant ships in a little extracurricular privateering. Well, when the king's political enemies used this against the king, he denied that Kidd was working for him and branded him a pirate."

"What happened then?"

"Kidd found out about it and sailed to Boston to straighten things out with Richard Coote, the governor, but Coote was in trouble himself, and he had Kidd jailed and sent back to England."

"That's dreadful," said Cassie. "I hope the king let him go."

"No. He had Kidd jailed. Then he was tried and convicted of piracy. They sent him to the gallows in 1701. Hanged him."

"That wasn't right!" exclaimed Cassie. "But what about all his treasure? What happened to that?"

"That's the mystery," said Mrs. Wentworth, eyes sparkling. "The New England authorities confiscated the bounty left by Kidd on Gardiners Island near Long Island Sound. But it didn't amount to much. Legend has it that some of the millions in gold and silver that Kidd pirated over the years is hidden along the Maine coast."

"You mean right here in Kittiwake Bay?" asked Cassie, wide-eyed.

"So the story goes," said Mrs. Wentworth. "My grandfather used to say he was sure of it. He searched for it, but never did find anything. Still, he was convinced the tunnels were a perfect hiding place for—"

The porch door crashed open, and Mr. O'Reilly, face flushed, hurried over to them. "Isabelle, I can't find it!" he cried. "It's gone! My beautiful chess set is gone!"

Chapter Eight

A week later, Cassie sat on the back step of the cottage, her arm draped over Sam, her hand stroking his bony head. "You're always here, Sam, to listen to my troubles," she murmured. Sam gave Cassie's cheek a wet kiss.

Long shadows from the woods fell across the lawn as the sun set behind them. As daylight faded and evening deepened, Cassie watched the trees mesh into a single dark mass.

The screen door swung open, and her mother stepped out. Cassie moved over to make room for her. Sam shifted, then settled himself comfortably, his face resting on his outstretched paws.

Her mother sighed. "We don't get much time to talk, do we, Cassie?" she said, resting her chin in her hands, her elbows on her knees.

"You're never here," said Cassie. She heard the accusation in her voice and felt ashamed. After all, her mother couldn't help it if she had to work so many hours.

After a small silence, Mrs. Hartt said, "You're looking kind of glum and you were rather sharp with Danny at supper. You two getting along all right?"

Cassie nodded, though Danny was a real pain some days, and on those days she wished her mother were around. "It's not Danny. It's just that I feel so bad for Mr. O'Reilly. He's still upset about his missing chess set."

"Maybe he misplaced it. Maybe it wasn't stolen."

"I don't think so, Mom. We looked everywhere." Cassie sighed. "I really like him and Mrs. Wentworth. Sometimes . . ."

"Sometimes what, Cass?"

Cassie glanced at her mother sideways. "Sometimes, I pretend they're my grandparents."

"Darn! There's the phone," said Mrs. Hartt, getting up to answer it. Cassie heard the murmur of her voice, then her returning steps. At the screen door, she said, "Someone called in sick. I have to work the evening shift. You'll be here for Danny, right?"

"I'll be here. Liz is coming over."

"Good. I'll go change."

A short time later, Cassie heard her talking to Danny, who was watching TV in the living room, then her quick footsteps in the kitchen. "Cass, did you see my keys?"

"On the counter. Near the toaster," Cassie hollered.

"Be sure Danny gets to bed on time," said her mother as the kitchen door slammed behind her. "I'll be late."

Watching her mother's old Ford disappear down the driveway, she wished she could have stayed home. Wished they could have talked more, like before—before the divorce.

"Penny for your thoughts," said Liz, rounding the side of the house.

"Oh, you've got the pictures!" Cassie cried, jumping to her feet and reaching for the envelope. "Maybe they'll cheer everybody up at Waterview."

Liz laughed. "I'm not sure about that. I think I need lessons on focusing. But some of them came out pretty good."

Cassie leafed through the packet of snapshots. "This one is great, Liz. How elegant Mrs. Wentworth looks. She'll love it! And Mr. O'Reilly and Mr. Johnson! You can tell by the expression on

Mr. O'Reilly's face that he's winning the checkers game."

Cassie went through the pictures a second time, then stopped to study one. "Who's that climbing the rocks?" she asked, holding out a picture of the cliff overlooking the bay.

Liz, tugging her braid, held the picture. "I think it's John Hudson, but it's hard to tell. I was aiming for a close-up of some flowers. I really need lessons on using this camera." She bent over and pulled the camera out of her bag. "How about posing for me with Sam? If you don't mind waiting, I should be able to get it in focus."

"Why don't you ask your father how to use it?"

"He never takes pictures."

"I thought it was his camera, that he'd loaned it to you."

Liz flushed, then looked Cassie in the eye. "Promise to keep a secret?"

Cassie crossed her heart. "Sure."

"Ryan gave it to me."

"Where did he get such an expensive camera?"

"He said it was his brother's, but he left home years ago. So Ryan said I could use it, but not to tell anyone."

Cassie chewed on her lip. "He was kind of quiet last night at the Sand Shack. Sometimes I think he doesn't like me. I wish Marc had been there."

"Ryan likes you, all right. Sometimes he gets moody and doesn't talk much. It's too bad Marc has two jobs now. But you must see him at Waterview."

"Not often. I'm usually gone by the time he gets there," Cassie said. "Can I take the pictures to the Waterview people?"

"Sure. Tell them they're a gift from me," said Liz, handing the pictures to Cassie. "Now, how about posing with lazy Sam?"

After Liz left, Sam lumbered to his feet, stretched, then walked sedately toward the woods. Sometimes he seems old like Mr. O'Reilly, Cassie thought. But other times, when he's tracking rabbits in those woods, he seems like a puppy again.

I wonder what did happen to Mr. O'Reilly's chess set. Who could have taken it? Cassie's thoughts continued to roam over happenings at Waterview Manor. Her throat constricted when she remembered being stuck in that stuffy closet. Who had slammed the door shut? John? Ryan? And why?

Bits and pieces of Mrs. Wentworth's stories flashed through her mind. Runaway slaves, the Underground Railroad, Captain Kidd's treasure.

The night had darkened the sky to a velvety

blackness. Lightning bugs flashed their tiny lights, briefly illuminating the dark. Like little signals, thought Cassie. Signals. Mrs. Wentworth had mentioned signals from the tower for the runaway slaves, and Cassie had seen a light flash from the tower her first night in town.

I wonder how many more times it's flashed since then . . . and why? It's time to find out. No matter how spooky those forbidden hallways are, I'm going to find a way to that tower.

Chapter Nine

A few nights later, Cassie concealed her bike behind a boulder by the side of Waterview Way, then darted from rock to rock toward the manor. She hid behind a wind-twisted fir, listening to the surging sea battering the jagged rocks far below. High in the purple-black sky loomed the tower, its glinting windows like giant eyes watching her. A chill shivered down Cassie's spine.

The screen door squeaked as she pushed it open and squeezed inside. She waited to see if anyone had heard it. Mrs. Sutton had made it clear that no one was to enter the closed-off portion of the house. But Cassie had to find out what was going on.

The atmosphere at Waterview Manor had changed. Mr. O'Reilly wasn't the only one who had lost something. Mrs. Burke's jewelry and Mr. Johnson's coin collection were also missing. Before, people had left their bedroom doors unlocked; now, they locked them. The friendly camaraderie among the residents was gone. They were quieter now and regarded one another with suspicion.

Cassie heard a murmur of voices from the porch, but saw no one in the dining room or hallway. Heart thumping, she slipped into the east wing.

She tiptoed along the uneven floor until she reached the door that warned NO TRESPASSING— EAST WING CLOSED. She pulled the door open, stepped inside and, after closing it behind her, clicked on her flashlight.

She walked lightly, trying not to make a sound. She knew if she continued straight, she would come to the farthest point of the east wing, where the wind sang its melancholy song. Since the tower rose from the center of the house, she turned into a central hallway.

Cassie flashed her light along the walls. Its beam showed doors on the right side. Halfway down the corridor was a narrow stairwell. She climbed the creaky stairs to the third floor.

Her footsteps echoed as she walked toward the front hallway, then turned left toward the center of the ancient house. She hoped she could find her way back. What if she missed the turn into this dark passage?

The moon cast an eerie glow through dirt-encrusted windows that shuddered in the wind. The air was stale and sour. Something scuttled by Cassie's feet. She drew back against the wall, her mouth dry, her heart pounding. A mouse, or maybe a rat, scurried across her light's pale beam, then vanished into the dark.

What am I doing here? she wondered, tempted to turn back. But she was so close. She had to find the tower.

Gripping the splintery railing, she climbed steep steps to the fourth floor. Mrs. Wentworth's voice echoed in her ears. "Oh, yes. I've been in the tower. You just open a door off the fourth floor and climb a stairway. It twists round and round, and when you reach the top, you can see the most magnificent views."

As Cassie pulled a door open, she heard a floorboard groan behind her. She froze, not daring to breathe, every nerve in her body prickling. Was someone following her? She listened intently. Nothing. No sound. She closed the door and moved on to the next one, trying to shake the feeling of another presence.

When she pulled the next door open, dusty air

made her sneeze. Her light showed ladderlike steps. The space was smaller than the linen closet, she thought, swallowing against the fear rising in her throat. But the door will be open behind me, and no one's going to close it. She peered into the shadowy hallway, then, turning sideways, climbed the cramped passage. A rope, knotted into iron rings along the wall, helped her pull herself up. As she rounded a twist in the staircase, something brushed against her face. She slapped it away and felt the splat of something soft against her hand. She shuddered and wiped her hand against her jeans. Above her, the darkness lightened, and soon she climbed up onto a wooden platform encircled by a low railing.

Eight arched windows, reaching from floor to ceiling, offered breathtaking views. The purple sky had deepened into black, and a brilliant moon shimmered over the sea and cast long shadows across the tower floor. The wind whistled shrilly through treetops and rattled the windows in their casements. A night bird flew by.

To the east, the sea crashed against the rocks, spewing columns of moonlit spray. Beyond the bay, and above Sail Street, stretched the woods. Those woods, Cassie thought, must lead to the Fairways' estate and our house. They're the woods

Sam is always running off to.

Cassie rotated her light slowly around the tower floor. There was no place to hide a signal light, but then, all someone would need was a flashlight. "The dust and grime have been disturbed, though," mused Cassie aloud, "and this window, the one facing the woods, is cleaner than the others."

"You're very observant," said someone stepping into the stairway.

"Marc!" Cassie cried. "I thought I heard footsteps before—it was you!"

Marc grinned. "Who did you think it was? A ghost?"

Cassie's eyes flashed. "You followed me! Why didn't you let me know you were there?"

"You looked very suspicious, Cassie, sneaking up here at night," said Marc, sounding defensive.

Cassie bristled. "Suspicious? Mrs. Wentworth told me how they used to signal from this tower when it was safe to bring in the runaway slaves, so I wanted to see it."

"Why at night? Why didn't you come up during the day?"

"I thought it would be easier to sneak in at night," said Cassie, glaring at him. "Anyway, once I saw . . ." She stopped.

"What did you see?" he asked sharply.

"Something," she mumbled, turning and looking out at the bay.

"A flashing light?"

Cassie wheeled and looked into his face. "You've seen it, too?"

Marc punched her arm lightly. "You're okay, Cassie. Coming up here at night when you think someone is sending signals from this tower. And I never really thought that you . . ." He stopped and grinned sheepishly.

"Thought that I what?" she asked. Noting his embarrassment, she gasped, "You were wondering if I was the thief."

"I guess we're all suspects here until the police find out who's guilty."

"The police?"

"Mrs. Sawyer called them after Mrs. Wentworth's lavaliere was stolen. She says the police will probably question all of us."

Cassie's heart gave a heavy thump. Mrs. Wentworth's treasured lavaliere. She sat down on the top step. "Poor Mrs. Wentworth. How is she? When did it happen?"

"Oh, that's right. You wouldn't know about it, since you didn't work today. It happened this morning, or sometime last night. You know how she puts it on the table right next to her bed? This morning, when she woke up, it was gone."

Cassie gazed out the window at the moon-gold bay. "It must be somebody who works here. Mrs. Wentworth never has visitors," she said. "Who was here last night?"

"John Hudson and Mrs. Sawyer were here till eleven, then Mrs. Collins, the night nurse. But it could be anyone. There are visitors for some of the other people back and forth all the time."

"John Hudson," mused Cassie. "I wonder . . ."

"John's harmless. A little slow, but harmless."

Cassie gnawed her lower lip. "I suppose you're right. But someone is taking these old people's treasures, and we've got to find out who."

"I thought you'd say that," said Marc, his voice thoughtful, his face in shadow.

"How come every time I search this old place, I come across you?" asked Cassie. "I bet you've been searching for that tunnel. The one Mrs. Wentworth says was used for the Underground Railroad or for Captain Kidd's treasure."

"I have done a little sleuthing on my own, but I haven't been able to find any tunnel," said Marc, stepping up onto the platform. "That cellar is immense and as black as a pit. And it's filled with all kinds of junk. I don't think anyone ever threw anything out. Just put it down in the cellar."

"I wonder," said Cassie, "if there's any connection between the robberies and the tunnel."

"You really think there is a tunnel?"

"Mrs. Wentworth seems so sure of it," said Cassie, rubbing her chin. "But let's do some research on our own. We could start with the library."

"Good idea. We'll go tomorrow," said Marc.

"Okay," said Cassie. "Tomorrow."

Chapter Ten

The next morning Cassie biked with Danny to the Beachcombers, then coasted down Sail Street to Waterview Way. Usually she looked forward to going to the Manor, but today she dreaded seeing Mrs. Wentworth. She knew how upset she would be.

Cassie found Mrs. Wentworth in her room. She sat in her wheelchair holding the small, velvet-lined box she had kept her lavaliere in. She looked up at Cassie with eyes full of pain. "They took my lavaliere, Cassie, my wedding gift from Hobart."

Cassie swallowed over the lump in her throat. "I know, Mrs. Wentworth. I'm sure the police will get it back."

"I wish I could be so sure." Mrs. Wentworth's

chest heaved, and she sighed. "I still have my memories, though," she said, her eyes sparkling a bit. "Nobody can take those away from me."

"And look, Mrs. Wentworth," Cassie said, opening a manila envelope and pulling out the pictures Liz had taken. "Liz sent these for you and Mr. O'Reilly and the others."

Mrs. Wentworth studied the pictures of herself. "They're not bad," she said, smiling. "Liz has a good eye for composition. This one is a little out of focus, though."

"She says she needs to work on that," Cassie said.

Mrs. Wentworth's eyes strayed from the pictures back to the empty box. From the porch, Cassie could hear the sound of voices as the residents claimed their favorite chairs for the day. Wanting to cheer Mrs. Wentworth, she said, "Tell me about when you were young, Mrs. Wentworth. What was it like here, then?"

Mrs. Wentworth handed her the pictures and sighed. "Beautiful, more wild. Many wealthy people summered here then. But my family lived here year-round. When I was a youngster, my mother, father, and I lived with my grandparents in a beautiful house on the coast. It wasn't as big as this place, but it was handsome." She stopped and pointed to her closet. "Be a dear, Cassie, and get me my photo album."

Cassie took a brown leather-covered album from the closet shelf and handed it to the old lady. With stiff fingers, she turned the frayed pages. "Here it is. Here's our house," she said softly.

Cassie crouched by her side and looked at a large, rambling house high on a cliff overlooking the ocean. "It is beautiful," she breathed.

Mrs. Wentworth turned more pages. "Here's this house in its heyday." She rested the book in her lap and gazed out the window. "Every Christmas, the Palmers hosted an elegant Christmas ball right here in the center hall. In my parents' day, candles glowed in chandeliers and in sconces along the walls. Garlands of greens and berries hung from the tall windows. And a great tree blazed with candlelight in the dining room.

"But by my early teens, they had installed kerosene fixtures. My father said it was a good thing, that the candles were a fire hazard, but I always imagined the candles were prettier. It was at a Christmas ball that I met Hobart." She looked down at a faded picture of herself and a young man dancing in the festive hall. "He was visiting relatives. We danced and danced. It seems like the musicians played Strauss waltzes all night long."

Cassie rested her cheek on the arm of Mrs. Wentworth's chair. "So that's why you like Strauss so much."

Mrs. Wentworth laughed a merry little laugh. "I always told Hobart that I fell in love with him and Strauss that night."

"It sounds so romantic." Cassie sighed, standing up. "When did they stop having the Christmas balls? What happened to the Palmer family?"

Mrs. Wentworth pressed her lips together and shook her head sadly. "The crash, Cassie. The great stock market crash of nineteen twenty-nine. Many people lost their money then, including the Palmers and my family. Things were never the same after that. But Hobart and I kept in touch, and after we finished school, we settled down here in Kittiwake to teach. And for a wedding gift he scraped and saved and gave me my beautiful rose lavaliere." She looked at the empty, velvet-lined box that Cassie had placed on her nightstand, and Cassie saw a tear slide down her cheek.

"How about some Strauss now, Mrs. Wentworth?" Cassie asked.

Mrs. Wentworth wiped her hand across her face. "That would be nice, Cassie," she said, buzzing her chair toward the door.

* * * *

Later that day, Cassie and Marc bent their heads over a small booklet entitled *A Short History of Kittiwake Bay, Maine.* Cassie flipped through pages about early settlers, the first meetinghouse, early wars, then stopped at a page captioned "Underground Railroad." The two of them skimmed the short passage rapidly, then Cassie read aloud:

"'. . . The Palmer Mansion, built in the mid-1800s, played a role in the Underground Railroad. Madison Palmer, who built the house, created a maze of tunnels to help runaway slaves. In the 1930s, the tunnel entrances were blocked for safety reasons.'"

Cassie and Marc looked at each other. "There really is a tunnel," said Cassie.

"More than one," said Marc. "But they closed them off."

"Maybe, but that was a long time ago. I bet you can still get through," said Cassie.

She leafed through the rest of the book. "It doesn't say anything about Captain Kidd's treasure."

"That happened way before the town was settled," said Marc. "Let's ask the librarian. Maybe she can refer us to another book."

The librarian, a tall, thin woman, said, "We do

have a book about treasure along the Maine coast. It's in the reference section and can't be taken out." She led them to a back shelf, her square heels clacking on the stone floor. "Somebody was in a few weeks ago asking for it. Every so often, there's an interest in Captain Kidd's treasure. Usually it's kids your age.

"Goodness, it's not here," she murmured. She pushed her glasses firmly into place and squinted at the book titles again. "It's gone. I wonder if that little man took it. I told him it couldn't leave the library."

"Little man?" said Cassie.

"Small and skinny. Older. Not a teenager. I remember him because he kept snapping a great wad of gum."

Chapter Eleven

Cassie was anxious to start searching for the tunnel, but she had to wait until Marc, who worked evenings, had the time off. Cassie felt she was going to burst with suspense. She was tempted to confide in Liz. But she and Marc had agreed not to tell anyone else about the secret tunnel. Finally, the day arrived.

"Cassie, you've hardly eaten a thing," said her mother.

"I'm just not hungry," said Cassie, pushing at a piece of chicken with her fork.

"She's daydreaming about Marc," said Danny, biting into his third chicken leg.

"What are you talking about?" asked Cassie, wide-eyed.

"I heard you and Liz. 'Marc and Ryan. Ryan and Marc.' Dumb girls' talk."

"That's enough, Danny," said their mother. "And don't talk with your mouth full."

"You've got big ears, Danny," said Cassie, her face burning. "But Marc is coming over in a little while, Mom. We're going for a bike ride."

"Can I come?" asked Danny, sitting up straight and as expectant as a puppy.

"No! Not this time, anyway," said Cassie. She pushed her chair back and started to clear the table.

"I never go anyplace, except the old Beachcombers," muttered Danny, slamming out the back door.

"I can't take him, Mom, really," said Cassie.

"No one said you had to," answered her mother, taking a cup of coffee and the mail into the living room.

Cassie squirted detergent into the sink and turned on the hot water. She washed and rinsed the dishes and put them in the drain for Danny to dry and put away. Danny. She certainly didn't want him tagging along. She and Marc wouldn't be able to go to Waterview Manor. But then, she thought, smiling, I wouldn't want Danny along, anyway. It wasn't really a date, of course. But,

84

still—Danny just couldn't go with them.

From the kitchen window, Cassie saw Marc wheel his bike into the backyard. Her heart raced in anticipation.

Marc rapped on the screen door.

"Come on in," said Cassie, drying her hands.

"Those brownies look good," said Marc, eyeing the plateful on the counter.

"Help yourself," said Cassie, sliding the plate toward him. "I'll be ready in a minute."

She came downstairs a short time later and heard Marc's deep laugh. He and Danny sat on the back step with the plate of brownies between them. Danny was giggling as they took turns tossing pieces to Sam, who jumped up and caught them in his mouth.

"You two really have old Sam moving around," said Cassie, laughing. "You'd think he was a puppy again."

She took a brownie and let Sam eat it from the palm of her hand. "Why don't you act your age, you silly," she said. Kneeling in front of the dog, she held his narrow face between her hands and kissed the top of his head. He slobbered a wet tongue across her face.

Cassie dried her cheek against her shoulder. "I'll put Sam in, then we can go," she said to Marc.

"Aren't you taking him with you?" asked Danny.

"No. Not tonight," said Cassie. She hoped Danny wouldn't think this was odd, since she always took Sam with her. Sometimes he even went to Waterview Manor with her to visit Mr. O'Reilly and the others.

"I'll take him in," said Danny.

Cassie eyed him dubiously. "I don't want him roaming away in those woods again," she said, frowning.

Danny thrust out his lower lip. "Leave him out, Cassie. I want to play with him. I'll bring him in."

Cassie hesitated, then said, "All right. But don't forget. I don't want him prowling around in those woods when I'm not here."

"You already said that, Cassie. And I won't forget. I'm not a baby, you know."

As Cassie and Marc started toward Fairway Drive, Danny called, "Don't forget, Marc, you said I could come next time you and Cassie go for a ride!"

Cassie felt the color rise to her face and hoped Marc didn't notice it. "Little brothers," she muttered.

"I know. I have one, too," said Marc, shrugging.

"Cassie. Marc. Hi," called Liz as she popped

through an opening in the hedge. "Where are you two off to?" she asked, catching up to them.

"Just a bike ride," said Marc, glancing at Cassie.

"I'd go with you, but I'm baby-sitting at the Fairways'. Ryan's going to call me. Maybe tomorrow we can all go to the Sand Shack. I'll ask him."

"Sounds good," Marc said.

"Talk to you tomorrow," Cassie said.

"Okay," Liz said, turning toward the Fairways'.

"Ryan's paying a lot of attention to Liz this summer," Marc murmured.

Cassie thought about the camera and Ryan's strange request that Liz not tell anyone. She looked at Marc out of the corner of her eye. "I think Liz likes him," she said.

"Well," said Marc. "I hope she doesn't get hurt."

"Get hurt? Why? Don't you think Ryan likes her? She's lots of fun . . . and a great friend."

"I know she is," said Marc. "We've known each other since kindergarten, but she's not the type Ryan usually goes for."

Halfway up Waterview Way, Cassie and Marc wheeled their bikes off the road. After hiding them behind a large boulder, they creeped toward the main entrance, hoping to enter unseen and slip in to the forbidden east wing. But as they got nearer, they realized that plan wouldn't work. Mr.

Johnson and his daughter had settled themselves in chairs on the front veranda, and there was Mrs. Sawyer, chatting with them.

"Now what do we do?" Cassie hissed to Marc.

Marc rubbed his chin and raised his eyebrows. "Are you game for a little climbing?"

"Sure," Cassie said, determined to find the tunnel.

"Follow me," Marc said. He bent low and, hidden by boulders and shrubs, led Cassie to the east side of the mansion. He stopped at the semicircular side porch.

"We can't get in that way!" Cassie said, looking up at the boarded windows and remembering her first exploration of the old house and the ghostly sound she had heard.

"No, not this way," said Marc. "Remember the balcony I showed you? There's a fire ladder that leads to it. But it's rickety." He paused, then said, "Maybe we should wait."

"No!" Cassie exclaimed. "We've come this far. Let's not turn back."

Marc looked into her eyes and grinned. "Okay, let's go!"

As Cassie sped from the protection of the boarded-up side porch, gusts of wind pushed against her. The boom of incoming breakers and the constant crying of seagulls crashed in her ears.

Above her, gray and white clouds raced across the sky. With luck, she thought, they would find the tunnel and be back while there was still light in the sky.

Cassie gripped the sides of the wobbly fire ladder. Her hands became numb as she climbed higher and higher. She didn't dare look down at the shelves of granite below.

She heaved herself up the last step onto the balcony. Now she turned to look down on the churning water spewing foam amidst jagged rocks. Letting out a shuddering breath, she followed Marc inside. Here, the rush of wind and sea was dulled. She rubbed her hands together to return the flow of blood. Her eyes, still tearing from the wind, adjusted to the dimness. The quiet of the deserted rooms closed around her.

Chapter Twelve

They stole down the stairs to the vestibule where Cassie had first heard the wind howling its mournful song. Her stomach tightened as she closed the cellar door behind them, and they descended the steep stairs to the belly of the house. The farther down they went, the stronger the musty damp odor grew. Their lights illuminated only a pale path in the cavernous cellar. Cassie rotated her flashlight from side to side. Innumerable objects cluttered the granite and dirt floor—tall, narrow chests, wicker rockers, trunks, hat stands, a rocking horse.

"According to that booklet, there's a tunnel that leads from the bay side to the house," Marc said, his voice sounding hollow.

"And from the house to the ocean," Cassie finished.

"Right. So there must be a tunnel entrance on the west side. Keep your light straight ahead. Don't flash it up," he cautioned.

"Why?" Cassie asked, immediately swinging the light upward. It showed great wooden beams that seemed to be moving. Cassie stared and focused the light on one spot. The beams were alive with shimmering hard-backed beetles. "Gross," she muttered, shielding her head with her hand.

"I told you not to look." Marc chuckled.

After what seemed an eternity to Cassie, they stood in the opposite side of the cellar. Here, there wasn't as much discarded furniture, but one huge chest loomed in front of them.

"Why do you suppose they pushed this heavy thing all the way down here?" Cassie wondered aloud. "Marc," she said, her voice rising with excitement, "this chest's been moved recently. You can see scratches on the floor!"

"You're right," Marc said, flashing his light on the floor. He circled to the back of the massive piece. "Take a look at this, Cassie! I didn't see this the last time I was here. The chest must have been on top of it."

"A trapdoor!" exclaimed Cassie, her light playing on the circular iron door in the floor. "Come on, let's go," she added, impulsively reaching for the iron ring.

"Hold it, Cassie," Marc said. "We might be getting into some real danger."

"I know," Cassie murmured. "But we have to find out what's going on, Marc. And I think this will lead us to the answer."

Marc nodded, and together they pulled open the trapdoor. Marc went down first, and Cassie followed, leaving the door open behind her. She didn't want to be closed in. They descended on slimy stone stairs farther into the center of the cliff. A heavy silence pulsed in Cassie's ears.

They stood in a tunnel about five feet across and six feet high. It branched in two directions. Cassie's light shone along the stone ceiling and wavered into a mysterious distance. She started down the sloping passage. "I have a feeling this leads to the ocean," she said.

"And the other direction must lead to the bay," said Marc, behind her. "That must be where they smuggled the runaway slaves in."

The air was heavy and humid. Cassie felt its weight clogging her throat. Her clothes stuck to her. The two proceeded in silence, concentrating on keeping their footing on the slimy, rock-strewn floor. Cassie shrieked when a rat scuttled past her and vanished in the coal-black tunnel.

The passageway grew narrower, and Cassie started breathing in shallow gasps. She stopped suddenly, and Marc bumped up against her.

"The tunnel seems to be blocked, Marc," she said in a shaky voice.

Marc reached for her hand in the darkness. Cassie was grateful for the warmth of his hand and stepped closer to him.

They played their lights on the low crawl way in front of them. The tunnel was not blocked, but it began to get much more narrow. "Do you want to turn back?" asked Marc.

"We've come so far. I guess that's big enough for us to crawl through," Cassie said. She drew in deep breaths to relieve the constricted feeling in her chest.

"Okay. You follow me," said Marc.

Tremors flitted down Cassie's spine as she got down on all fours. Small pieces of rock bit into her palms and knees. Her light bobbed erratically, briefly illuminating the sole of Marc's sneaker, then jerking upward.

Her palm squished on something, and she focused her light on it. Stuck to her hand was the body of a dead cricket, encased in a shroudlike mold. She screamed and scraped her palm against a rock so hard, it started to bleed.

Marc stopped. "You okay, Cassie?"

"No. I want to get out of here," she said, close to tears.

"Come on," said Marc in a calm voice. "We'll be able to stand up in a minute."

Through sheer will, Cassie followed Marc until they could finally stand. Marc put a comforting arm around Cassie's shoulders as she got shakily to her feet.

"I'm sorry to be such a baby," Cassie apologized. "I felt like I couldn't breathe."

"I don't much like this place myself," said Marc. "I hope there's another way back."

A short time later, they rounded a bend, and the darkness lightened. Cassie could hear the faint swish of water.

"Thank heavens," said Cassie, quickening her step.

They passed a cluster of freestanding rocks and stood in a cave about ten feet high. Ebbing light suffused the entrance and dimmed toward the back, where rocks and small boulders filled the floor.

Cassie walked out of the cave and looked in

wonder at an awesome scene. Above and behind her rose the great granite cliff, where a Kittiwake called and darted into its nest. To Cassie's left and right rose high, perpendicular walls of rock. They circled and formed an almost solid wall, but straight ahead was an opening no more than six feet wide. She could hear the muted sound of giant waves crashing against the seaward side of the cliff. In front of her, enclosed within the granite walls, a small lake of seawater rose quietly, liquid gold from lingering sun rays.

"Cassie," Marc called, "you've got to see this." Cassie rushed back to where Marc stood in the center of the cave, playing his light into its dark interior. "Fresh digging. Someone's been searching for something."

"The treasure!" cried Cassie, her eyes sparkling. "Do you think it's here, or did somebody already find it?"

They flashed their lights on the rock-and-clay floor. A pickax lay discarded amidst small piles of earth. Farther back, another room branched off the main one. Cassie ducked and followed Marc through the low entrance.

The feeble rays of their lights barely penetrated the thick darkness. Cassie swallowed hard and reached for Marc. His comforting arm went around her shoulders, and he pulled her close.

Their revolving lights showed the cave to be the size of a small closet. It was dry and empty. "If there was any treasure, it's gone now," Marc said.

Cassie slowly played her light along the floor of the suffocating space. Something flashed and sparkled in the probing beam. She knelt and picked up an emerald earring lying amidst a pile of small stones. Its deep green glowed luminously.

Cassie closed her hand around the jewel. "Come on, Marc, let's get out of here."

In the main cave, she opened her hand and stared at the emerald. "This certainly isn't part of Captain Kidd's treasure. It's much too modern."

"Wow," exclaimed Marc, looking at the earring. "I think we're on to something. And look at this." He knelt and examined some marks on the floor. "Something heavy's been kept here and dragged through the cave."

"A boat. I bet it was a boat," said Cassie, dropping the earring into her pocket. "It's all beginning to make sense. Come see the secret lake. You'll see what I mean."

They walked from the cave to the edge of the shimmering water. "Cool," Marc breathed.

"Isn't it fantastic?" said Cassie. "Who would ever believe it was here? From the back of the mansion, looking down, all you can see are waves crashing in."

"It must be because of the rock formation. And this is a very narrow area," said Marc.

"Look how rapidly the water is rising. Do you think it will flood the cave?" Cassie asked nervously.

"Never," said Marc. "The cave's above high-tide level. Any moisture in there would be from the sea air or a driving rain. Besides, there's no sand on the floor."

"What does that mean?" asked Cassie.

"If water filled the cave at high tide, it would leave sand behind. No sand, no water. Also, there's no discoloration of the walls. If the sea rose into the cave, it would discolor the walls," Marc explained.

"You're sure?" said Cassie, looking at the swiftly rising water.

"Positive. This must be how they got the runaway slaves out. They hid a boat in the cave. Got the people through the tunnel. Then, at high tide, or just as the tide turned, they could push off. A good navigator could get through that gap in the cliff wall. I bet you can barely see that from the ocean side."

"And that must be what the thieves of

Kittiwake are doing," said Cassie, fingering the jewel in her pocket. "Only, instead of helping runaway slaves, they're helping themselves to other people's things."

"And maybe Captain Kidd's treasure," said Marc.

The sun sank lower, taking its light from the sea lake. Cassie looked at the now leaden water and shivered. "I guess we have to go back through that tunnel," she whispered. "There's no other way."

"What a relief to be out in the air again," Cassie cried. She stooped and immersed her bleeding and throbbing hand into the cool ocean water that washed against the beach along Shore Road. She looked up at Marc and laughed. "I'll have to tell my mother we fell in the ocean, I guess."

"We are kind of damp," Marc said, drying his hands on his soiled T-shirt before they headed back toward their bikes.

When they turned down Fairway Drive, they stopped short, their brakes squealing. A police car with flashing lights stood in front of the Fairways'. Another car whizzed by them and braked in front of the house. Cassie and Marc sped down the road and reached the car just as Mr. and Mrs. Fairway jumped out.

"My baby! Where is my baby?" cried Mrs. Fairway.

"The baby's fine. He's with Liz Painter at the Hartts' cottage. They're both fine. The girl used good sense taking the baby out of the house as soon as she knew someone had broken in," said a policeman.

The Fairways, Cassie, and Marc dashed to the cottage. Inside, Jean Hartt and Danny were playing with the baby while a policeman talked to Liz.

Mrs. Fairway swept the cooing, smiling baby into her arms and held him so close, he started to cry. The policeman talked to the Fairways, then asked them to return to their house with him. They left, and Mrs. Hartt went into the kitchen to make hot cocoa.

Liz, her voice shaky, her eyes big and round, told Cassie and Marc what had happened.

"After the Fairways left, I checked all the doors and windows, you know, because of the robberies. Then I checked on the baby; he was sound asleep in his crib. Then I watched TV for a while. I was about to check on Christopher again when Ryan called. While we were talking, I thought I heard something, but Ryan teased me . . . said I was letting my imagination run away. We talked a little longer, then I went upstairs to check the baby."

Liz shuddered and tented her fingers against her head. "I knew right away something was wrong. The door to Mr. and Mrs. Fairway's room was closed and it had been open before. I could see into the baby's room from the hall light, and I saw him in his crib. I grabbed him and ran over here."

Cassie put her arms around Liz's trembling shoulders. "Good thinking, Liz," she said.

"It certainly was," Jean Hartt said. "Now drink your cocoa and have some cookies, then we'll walk you home."

They sat silently, sipping the cocoa. Cassie wondered if they were all thinking the same thing. What would have happened if the thief had seen Liz? If Liz had seen the thief? She put down her cup and said, "Marc and I will walk Liz home, Mom."

"Thanks," said Liz. "Suddenly the yards and hedges seem scary."

"I can't believe how quiet Sam is," Cassie said. "Where is he? He usually wants to be in on all the excitement."

Danny, who had been listening to Liz, bug-eyed and openmouthed, slipped out of his chair and started to leave the room.

"Danny. Where's Sam?" Cassie demanded.

Avoiding Cassie's eyes, Danny mumbled, "He didn't want to come in."

"Oh, Danny, you promised. I bet he went into the woods," Cassie said, frowning.

Outside, Cassie, Marc, and Liz headed for the woods, calling for Sam. Danny followed, saying over and over, "He wouldn't come in, Cassie. He wouldn't come in."

"Sam. Sam. Come on, boy. Come on," called Cassie. The underbrush rustled and parted, and Sam stumbled toward them.

"What's the matter with him?" cried Cassie. "He can't walk straight."

"He looks drunk!" said Danny.

Sam staggered to Cassie and collapsed at her feet.

"Tell your mom to get the car," yelled Marc, scooping the weak dog into his arms. "We'd better get Sam to a vet."

Chapter Thirteen

Cassie tossed and turned, drifting in and out of sleep. Half dreams disturbed her—dark tunnels, secret lakes, police cars with flashing lights, and Sam collapsing at her feet.

Morning broke, and she lay dozing, waiting for Sam to nuzzle her fully awake. Realization flooded through her, and she sat up quickly. Her head ached, and she felt a heavy sense of loss. Sam might be dead.

They had rushed him to the veterinarian, Dr. Eileen Casey. After examining Sam, the doctor had told them the dog was having a seizure. "Could he have gotten into some poison—strychnine?" she had asked. "That causes seizures like this. I'll keep him sedated. It's vital we stop these seizures."

"Will he be all right?" Cassie's throat was tight with unshed tears, and her voice had been barely audible.

"I hope so," the doctor had said kindly. "You got him here before he had a severe seizure. But he's old. I don't know about his heart. . . ." And her voice had trailed off.

Remembering those final words, Cassie hurried down the stairs to the phone and called Dr. Casey. Heart thumping, she waited for her to answer.

"Dr. Casey, is Sam all right?" Cassie's voice was a whisper. She cleared her throat and asked again.

She listened intently, nodded several times, then hung up the phone and turned to find Danny watching her. His eyes were big and round, his freckles dark on his pale face. "Is Sam dead?" he asked in a thin voice.

Cassie clenched her fists and choked back a sob. "No, he's not dead. Not yet, anyway. No thanks to you!"

Danny, a pleading look in his eyes, cried, "I'm sorry, Cassie! I'm sorry I didn't bring Sam in."

"Sorry won't help, Danny. I never should have trusted you. If Sam dies, it's all your fault."

Danny turned and ran, sobbing, up the stairs.

"Cassie, Danny didn't do anything on purpose,"

said her mother, coming in from the kitchen. "I don't understand why you didn't put Sam in before you left. You've always taken such good care of him."

"Oh, sure. It's up to me to take care of everybody! Ever since we moved here I've had to take care of Danny. Now look what he's done to Sam!" Cassie buried her face in her hands and burst into tears.

Her mother put her arms around Cassie's shoulders, and Cassie leaned against her. "What did the doctor say, Cass?"

Cassie struggled for control. "She said Sam's very weak. That the seizures have stopped, but he's very weak. She won't know for a few days if he'll make it or not."

"Oh, Cass, I know how you feel. I know how much you love Sam, but don't make matters worse by blaming Danny."

Cassie pulled away from her mother and flew up the stairs, shouting, "You don't know how I feel. Nobody does."

Cassie biked with Danny to the Beachcombers, not speaking a word, then rode farther up Sail Street to the veterinarian's. Sam lay on his side, dozing, an intravenous solution dripping into a vein in his front left leg. Cassie stroked his silky head, and he made small whimpering sounds.

She left the animal hospital choking back tears. Dr. Casey had said Sam definitely had gotten into strychnine. Cassie was more determined than ever to find out what was going on in Kittiwake Bay. Somebody had poisoned her dog, and she wanted to know why.

She biked home and sat on the back step to wait for Marc. They had decided last night to meet and make plans. Soon Marc rode into the yard and propped his bike against a tree.

"Hi, Cassie, how's Sam?" he called, pushing back his sweaty hair.

"They're still sedating him," Cassie answered. "The doctor won't know for a few days. Marc, I know we were planning to find out where the tunnel comes out on the bay side, but I'd rather explore the woods. I want to find out what happened to Sam."

"And you want to do it now," Marc said, grinning.

"I guess you're getting to know me," Cassie said, smiling weakly.

"Impulsive, impatient Cassie. Come on. The woods it is."

The day was overcast and airless. Cassie and

Marc ducked under an overhanging branch and stepped into the woods behind the garage. Heavy, humid air, smelling of pine needles, hung among the evergreens.

They walked farther into the quiet woods. Cassie kept her eyes to the ground, searching the floor of the forest, where wintergreen and bunchberry poked through spruce needles, for clues. It didn't take long.

"Here it is," said Cassie. She put her hand to her mouth, trying to still the retching that quivered through her. Dead flies and ants encrusted a dark mass lying near a patch of bunchberry. A few flies buzzed loudly, languorous, barely moving.

"A meat bone," Marc said, squatting down to inspect it.

"So Sam was poisoned on purpose," said Cassie.

Marc poked at the mass with a stick. "It looks that way. Let's leave it here for now. Later, we'll take it to Dr. Casey and have it checked for strychnine," he suggested.

Cassie looked away from the gory mess and forced herself to concentrate on the task at hand. "Whoever broke into the Fairways' wanted these woods to himself," she said. "I'm not sure why, but . . ." Thoughts tumbled through Cassie's mind. "Marc, the first time I came in here, I stepped on a wad of gum. Freshly chewed. So someone had been here just before me. And remember the flashing light I told you I saw from the tower? I think . . ."

Marc, interrupting, said excitedly, "And the clean pane of glass in the tower window faces the woods above Sail Street, these woods!"

"Let's go," said Cassie, starting in the direction of Sail Street.

"We'd better be quiet," cautioned Marc. "What if—"

"Right," said Cassie, her face somber. She knew what he was thinking. There could be someone else in the woods right now. Someone they wouldn't want to meet.

They stuck several sticks around the bone and covered it with stones, then started toward the ocean, trekking through stands of white pine and red spruce. Cassie's nerves were taut, her senses alert. Every sound seemed magnified a thousand times. High above her, the treetops stirred in a rustle of sea air. Small, redbreasted nuthatches whisked from tree trunks to litters of needles, chittering faintly to each other. A white-breasted nuthatch honked noisily. A red squirrel chattered as it leaped from tree to tree. She thought of Sam and of how his ears perked up and his nose twitched at the sounds and smells of these woods.

"Somebody's been through here recently," whispered Marc, pointing to a freshly broken branch above trampled leaves.

They moved closer together and followed the faint signs of a path up a steep incline. Cassie grabbed a branch to keep from sliding back on slippery pine needles.

A sea mist floated in as they got closer to the ocean. Cassie felt as though the fog were creeping over her, smothering her. They topped the rise and stood in a stand of balsam fir. Suddenly, they heard the sound of voices—muffled and angry. They stood frozen to the spot. Cassie's heart thumped loudly in her chest, and her mouth felt cottony dry.

The voices came nearer, and twigs cracked under the tread of feet. Cassie and Marc ducked behind a mammoth old tree. Cassie held her breath, not daring to breathe. Peering around the tree, she saw, not more than fifteen feet away, two mist-enshrouded figures—one tall, the other short, thin, and bowlegged.

"Hold it, Jake. I've got to get this stone out of my shoe. It feels like a boulder," said the taller man, kneeling and unlacing his shoe.

"You're sure you covered the entrance, Sailor?" asked the man called Jake. He chewed on a large wad of gum, snapping it loudly. He was wearing jeans and a red T-shirt.

"You were right there, Jake. Why didn't you check it yourself if you don't think I know what I'm doing? Sheesh. You sound like a cow with that gum."

Cassie studied the kneeling figure in the gloomy half-light. His jeans and open-neck shirt were a faded blue.

"I really don't think it was necessary for me to come into town, Jake. You know I can't take a chance of anyone recognizing me."

"No one saw you, Sailor. And I just wanted you to check things out on this end. I don't like those two kids nosing around. They've been snooping around in that tower, and I wouldn't be surprised if they're looking for the tunnel. If they find it and call the police . . ."

"Cool it, Jake. Why would they call the police?" asked Sailor, shaking the stone from his shoe. "It's just a tunnel. There's nothing there right now. We cleaned everything out."

"Yeah. I know. I know. But with that dog in these woods all the time, and that brat of a girl in here looking for him . . ."

"Well, you took care of the dog, and we transfer the stuff out of here next week. Wednesday night will be our last run. I told the boys in New York this town is just about cleaned out. Anyway, it's time to blow this backwater once and for all," said Sailor bitterly. "Now . . . do you have everything straight?"

"I've got the plan," said Jake, snapping his gum. "I wait for the signal, any time from eight o'clock on—then start carrying the stuff through. The kid meets me with the loot from Waterview, and we bring it all out to you."

Sailor took off his other shoe and shook it out. Looking up at Jake and wagging a finger to emphasize his words, he said, "And as soon as you see the signal, make tracks. Don't forget, I sail with the tide."

"Yeah, I know. I got it straight," grumbled Jake.

"Timing is important," said Sailor. "We're clearing everything out on Wednesday. Nothing gets left. And not a moment too soon with those kids snooping around, sticking their noses into every nook and cranny of that old mansion. When you get the signal, you'll know it's safe."

"When do I get my cut?"

"Not until the stuff's been fenced. That's the deal," said Sailor, tying his shoes and heaving himself to his feet.

Cassie and Marc didn't move for a full five minutes after the men left. Finally, the sounds of the men's noisy retreat faded, and Cassie could hear only the twitter of birds and the rustle of small animals.

"Now I know who poisoned Sam," she said in a tight voice, clenching her fists.

Marc patted Cassie's shoulder awkwardly. "I'm sure Sam will be all right," he said.

"Marc," said Cassie, looking straight into his blue eyes, "who do you suppose the 'kid' is who's meeting Jake?"

Marc stared back into Cassie's gray-green eyes, then looked away as though embarrassed. "Well, there's you, me, and Ryan. And I guess you could call John Hudson and the two night aides 'kids.'"

Cassie shuddered, thinking of John Hudson and the way he always stared at her. Then she remembered that rainy night and the man she saw talking to Jake. Could it have been Ryan? she wondered.

Denying the thought, she changed the subject. "Let's see if we can find the entrance they were talking about. I bet it leads to another tunnel that connects with the one leading to the secret lake."

They continued up the steep incline until they reached the edge of the woods near the Beach-combers' cottage. They looked down on Sail Street and out across the bay, gray under low clouds and sea mist. "We must have missed whatever entrance they were talking about," Marc said, running his hands through his hair.

The peal of a hermit thrush sounded in the dark distance of the woods behind them. Cassie, hot and tired, hesitated, then, turning to retrace their steps, said, "Let's check once more."

"We could scoot down to the Sand Shack and get a cold soda," Marc suggested.

Cassie licked her lips. It sounded good. Then she thought of Sam. Just up the street past the Beachcombers, he lay sick and still. "One more check," she insisted. Lifting her heavy ponytail to cool her neck, she headed back into the thick woods.

"I sure could use a soda," Marc said, sighing.

A short distance into the woods, going down a sharp incline, Cassie tripped on a tree-root and lost her balance. Stumbling, she fell to her knees and saw, nearly hidden in the pine needles, a flash of yellow. She bent and picked it up. "Marc, look at this. A gum wrapper. It's got to be that little man's—Jake's. The entrance must be around here someplace."

Cassie crept under low-hanging branches. Pine needles clung to her clothes and the palms of her hands. The trees stood close together here, their

112

heavy branches sweeping the ground. It was impossible to stand up without becoming entangled in them. Cassie was about to turn around and crawl back when her hand brushed something cold and hard.

"Marc! It's a trapdoor. Like the one in the cellar of the mansion."

Marc crept to her side, and together they brushed the needles from the metal door. He drew back a makeshift wooden bolt and lifted it.

A black hole yawned before them. Slowly, their eyes adjusted to the inky darkness, and they could discern ladderlike steps. A chill shivered down Cassie's spine.

Marc started down the steps and disappeared into the pit. Cassie waited. A lone raven croaked from a treetop.

"Cassie. Come on down. There's quite a cache in here and lots of flashlights."

Cassie looked around nervously.

"Cassie!" Marc's voice floated up from the pit.

Cassie peered down at him. His upturned face floated eerily in shadowy light.

"Cassie. Wait till you see what's down here! Don't worry, it's pretty roomy. Come on."

"What if they come back?" Cassie whispered, glancing over her shoulder.

"They're not coming back," Marc scoffed.

Cassie hesitated, then slid into the pit, feeling for the first step with her foot. *So long as the door is open,* she chanted in her head. *So long as the door is open.*

"It's probably a good idea," said Marc as Cassie dropped into the tunnel beside him, "to close the door, though, just in case. . . ." He clambered up a few steps, grabbed the ring in the center of the heavy lid, and pulled it down. It fell into place with a clang.

Cassie's heart plunged into her stomach. She felt entombed in the center of the earth. She reached for Marc's warm, strong hand. Marc played his light around the secret room and settled on a box full of flashlights. "Guess they don't like the dark, either," he said, handing one to Cassie. She switched hers on and saw that they stood in a hollowed-out circular room about five feet in diameter. The earthen walls had been reinforced with rough-hewn beams of wood that were now rotted in places. A narrow opening suggested a passageway.

"This must be where the runaway slaves hid," Cassie said with a shudder. "Just imagine. Traveling hundreds of miles, sometimes with nothing to guide them except the North Star, then having to climb down into this dark pit."

"But someone would bring them food. And they were almost free. Just a little farther to Canada," Marc said, sweeping his hand in an imitation of Mrs. Wentworth.

"But look what's here now!" he said, leading her to a deep ledge on one side. Their lights played over its contents—metal and cardboard boxes, and plastic-encased bundles. A fat-bodied black spider scurried away.

Marc reached in and lifted the lid of a metal box.

Cassie gasped in disbelief. Light rays refracted from a jumble of jewelry—rings, earrings, pins, necklaces—set with diamonds, sapphires, emeralds, rubies. "It's like a treasure chest," she breathed.

"But it's not Captain Kidd's treasure. It must be all the jewelry that's been stolen in town. And figurines, silver, cameras, some small electronics . . ."

Cassie rummaged through the jewelry. "I don't see Mrs. Wentworth's lavaliere," she murmured. "What's in these plastic bundles?" She reached in and pulled a small seascape from its protective covering. Suddenly, she heard an angry shout from above, then the sounds of someone struggling with the trapdoor.

"Come on," Marc whispered, pulling her deeper

into the dim passage that led from the room. "And turn off your light."

Cassie's eyes stretched wide against immediate blackness. As they scurried down the descending passage, she heard the opening whoosh of the trapdoor and Jake's sullen muttering.

Cassie hardly felt the bumps and scratches on her arms and legs. She only knew she didn't want Jake to find them. If he was capable of poisoning an innocent animal, what would he do to two kids? A stone rattled away from Cassie's foot. She and Marc stopped and backed against the wall, hoping Jake hadn't heard it.

"Who's there?" Jake cried. A stream of light flowed into the tunnel, stopping just short of Cassie. She shrank farther back against the wall. "Probably a rat," Jake mumbled.

Cassie felt Marc's arm slip reassuringly around her shoulders. She listened to Jake rummage through the stolen goods, heard him climb the stairs, shut the door with a thud, and draw the bolt.

Cassie's nerves—like cold wires running through her—tightened. She and Marc were locked into a hole in the earth. No one knew where they were.

Marc clicked his light on. Its beam faded in the

distance. "This tunnel must lead to the mansion," he said in a level voice.

Cassie swallowed, then, her voice a whisper, a prayer, said, "Yes. It must."

Chapter Fourteen

Cassie's light wavered. Its beam touched the wall, then glanced off rough-hewn, ladderlike steps that led farther down. She and Marc slipped and slid down the almost vertical passage. The downgrade ended, and Cassie stumbled into Marc. His arms went around her, and he hugged her reassuringly. "Don't worry, Cassie. We'll get out of here. We must be under Sail Street now, heading for the bay side."

Cassie leaned against him. She heard water dripping from the rocky ceiling and splashing in shallow puddles. The fetid, moist air was suffocating. Something scuffled and squealed by her feet. She shrieked and clutched Marc.

Marc's weak light caught the tail of a rodent

scurrying away. "It's just a rat," he said. His light dimmed, then momentarily brightened before it died. He shook it. Its tinny rattle sounded loud in the silence, but the light didn't go back on. Marc tossed the flashlight down, and it rolled away with a clatter.

"Cassie, let me take your light. Stay close behind me."

"I can't stand this place," Cassie said with a shudder. Reluctantly, she gave up her light and followed Marc through the narrow passage. His phantomlike figure seemed to float in front of her. Silence, except for the tread of their feet, the drip of water, the occasional scurrying of a rat.

The faint light disappeared into the curve of the passageway. Cassie's breathing was shallow. Her face felt hot and flushed, her hands icy. Would they ever get to the end of this tunnel and out into the fresh air? What if they couldn't get out? What if they had to turn back?

After what seemed an eternity, the granite floor beneath their feet sloped upward. They climbed the now ascending, now level passageway. Finally, Cassie smelled a delicious draft of fresh air. Anxious to flee the tunnel, she tread on Marc's heels.

"Here's where we get out," Marc said, grabbing her hand and playing the diminished light across a slab of granite that lay at an angle in front of them.

On either side of the leaning slab, light and fresh currents of salty air streamed in. Cassie peered through the left gap, no more than ten inches wide, but a way out.

"This side looks easier to get through," Marc said from her right. "It's a little wider."

"I can see why they have Jake using this tunnel and not the big guy, Sailor," Cassie said.

"Careful, Cassie. There're a lot of loose stones," warned Marc, squeezing through the opening. "They really piled a lot of rock in here to close off the tunnel."

"And Jake and Sailor and someone else have cleared a way through," said Cassie. A rock snagged her T-shirt as she scrambled after Marc. She wrenched free, tearing the cloth, and staggered out into the open air.

They were on a narrow ledge about halfway up the cliff that overlooked the bay. Cassie raised her face to the late afternoon sky, where slivers of blue were showing through the cloudy mass. A warm breeze caressed her face. She smelled and tasted the salty tang of the sea. She breathed deeply, filling her lungs with sweet fresh air. Then, glancing down at the bay, a flash of red caught her eye.

"Marc, get down. Quick," she cried, pulling

on his shirt. "Someone's looking up here."

"You certainly have sharp eyes," said Marc, squinting down at the bay.

"Get down," Cassie urged.

They flung themselves down onto their bellies on the scant ledge. Cassie pressed herself into the harsh stones beneath her, hoping to disappear, like a small animal, into the ground. "That's Jake down there," she whispered, her throat dry.

"I thought so. I can make out his red T-shirt and those bowlegs," said Marc.

They lay still, staring down through a scraggly bush that clung to its rocky bed. Cassie's cheek rested against her ice-cold hand. The figure below walked closer to the base of the cliff. Cassie noted the small boats bobbing about in the bay. As though in a nightmare, the wheeling, screaming seagulls seemed to mock her relief at having escaped the tunnel.

Jake climbed to a jutting rock about halfway up the cliff. He stood very still, staring upward. Cassie could see his dark brows drawn into a frown. She drew in her breath when she saw him grasp a bush to pull himself up to the next rock. The bush gave way with a tearing sound, and Jake tumbled back to the rocks. His angry shout rose on the air. He brushed himself off, then left, jumping from rock to rock. Cassie let her breath out slowly and felt the tension drain from her shoulders as she watched him disappear down Sail Street.

"I sure sweated that one out," Marc said, scrambling to his feet and slapping gravelly stones from his jeans. "You know, Cassie, there must be another tunnel. One that leads to the cellar and the secret lake. That would explain how the thieves are getting everything out of town.

"They hide the stolen goods in the tunnel room in the woods, and later, when it's safe, they take them to the cave lake. Then, when it's high tide, the man called Sailor must take everything out in a boat."

Cassie looked up at Waterview Manor. "They must find out when it's safe to transfer the stolen goods from here to the next tunnel by a signal from the tower," she mused. "From here, you can't see the whole house, but you can see the tower. That must be what happened my first night in Kittiwake. I saw that flashing light before I went into the store. And later, when I went over to look at the house, I heard men talking. They must have been taking the stolen goods to the cave."

"Are you game to try to find the other entrance?" Marc asked, his voice a challenge.

Cassie, raising an eyebrow and pursing her lips, looked at him in disbelief.

Marc chuckled. "Why don't we see if we can find the entrance but not go in? We're pretty sure there's another tunnel that leads to the cellar. If we find the entrance, we'll know we're right."

"Deal. We find the entrance, but we don't go in," Cassie agreed, holding out her hand.

"Deal," Marc said, grinning as they shook hands.

The late afternoon, though overcast, remained hot and muggy. As they inched along the meager ledge, Cassie glanced down over her shoulder every so often, afraid she might see Jake's bow-legged figure scampering up the cliff after them.

Even from a distance, they recognized the entrance. The ledge widened before a slab of granite set at an angle, surrounded by boulders and rocks. Cassie and Marc climbed over the scattered rocks. Cassie peered behind the leaning slab into yawning blackness. Her stomach lurched and her heart thumped loudly in her chest. "Never again," she vowed. "I'll never go in another tunnel."

Marc put his arm around her shoulders and gave her a squeeze. "Okay. We've found it. Let's go back now."

Cassie checked her watch. "It's almost time for me to meet Danny at the Beachcombers. I might as well just walk up there since we're so close. There's no sense in going all the way home to get my bike."

"I'll go with you," Marc said. "You know," he mused, looking up and along the side of the cliff, "we're about three-quarters of the way to Waterview Manor from here, so this leg of the tunnel must be pretty short."

Cassie had turned and started back down the ledge. "I don't care how short it is," she said fiercely. "I'm never going in it."

Soon she was standing on the stone Jake had recently stood on. "I'm roasting," she called up to Marc. She scampered down to the base of the cliff and jumped off the last rock onto the hard-packed shore, where the surging sea left long chains of white foam. Cassie lifted her face to the breeze and ran along the beach, arms outstretched, shouting, "We're free! Free as the gulls! Free as the fish we rescued!"

"You're crazy," Marc shouted, laughing and running to catch her.

Cassie raced up the incline from the bay to Sail Street, Marc chasing her. He caught her by the arm and pulled her toward him, holding her in a tight hug. Cassie felt his lips on her hair as he laughed and murmured, "You're one crazy girl."

Thrills of warmth rushed through her. She pulled back, exhilarated, laughing. Suddenly wary, she tensed and, turning, looked across the street. John Hudson stood in front of the Sand Shack. Ice cream dripped down his cone, over his hand, as he stared at them.

"Hey, John, your ice cream's melting," called Marc. "Come on, Cassie," he said, not waiting for a reply, "let's get Danny." He took her arm and turned her away from John, toward the Beachcombers' cottage.

"Marc. What do you suppose John was doing around here? Do you think he met Jake?"

"Um . . . no, I don't think so."

"Why not? You're always sticking up for him."

"I'm not sticking up for him. I just don't think he'd be involved in anything like this. He's not a bad guy."

Hand in hand, they trudged up Sail Street in silence. Soon they were below the rocky ledge that jutted out over the road. Looking up at the dark, close-growing evergreens, Cassie thought of the tunnel beneath them. And of Jake. That horrid little man who had poisoned Sam. Poor Sam. He just had to be all right!

"Will we be on time for Danny?" Marc asked, breaking the silence.

Danny, Cassie thought, the muscles in her face tightening. Then, her voice hard, she said, "It's all Danny's fault Sam is sick. Maybe dying. If it weren't for him, Sam wouldn't have been poisoned!"

Marc ran his fingers through his hair. "Cassie, Danny was really upset last night. He feels terrible about Sam. Don't be too tough on him."

Cassie pulled her hand from Marc's and glared at him. "Now you sound like my mother. Why are you taking Danny's side too?"

Marc frowned. "I'm not taking sides, Cassie. What happened was an accident."

Cassie clenched her hands. The joyous feeling of Marc putting his arms around her and brushing her hair with his lips was forgotten. "You heard him promise he'd get Sam in. You heard him say, 'I'm not a baby. I won't forget,'" Cassie said, her voice clipped.

"But he's just a little kid, Cassie. And it wasn't his fault there was poisoned meat in the woods."

"No. But it was his fault Sam was there to eat it!"

"You're being unreasonable, Cassie."

"Unreasonable? How . . . ?" Cassie stopped short when they rounded the bend to the Beachcombers' Playhouse, and saw the children clustered around Mrs. Antonelli. Even from the road, they could hear her unusually stern tone. "Don't ever talk to

126

strangers," she admonished. "And never take anything from them."

The wide-eyed children stared up at her solemnly. Danny and two other boys shifted uncomfortably. Then Danny spotted his sister. "Here's Cassie," he cried, turning from the group, "I have to go now."

"I was warning the children about strangers," explained Mrs. Antonelli to Cassie and Marc. "There was a man around here this afternoon talking to Danny and some of the other children."

"He just gave us gum," Danny said, "but Mrs. Antonelli took it away." He darted a quick look at Cassie. "Hey, Cassie, where's your bike?"

Cassie started to ask Mrs. Antonelli about the stranger, but she had turned to talk to a little girl's mother.

Danny dashed to get his bike and wheeled it over to Cassie and Marc. He pulled a notice from the bike basket and waved it at Cassie.

"There's going to be a big Labor Day picnic. Mrs. Antonelli says the whole town goes. Do you think Mom will go, Cassie?"

Cassie choked back her anger. "Maybe," she said. "If she doesn't have to work."

"Everybody goes. You'll go, won't you, Cassie?"

"I may have to work, too." Her words were short and curt.

"Oh," Danny said flatly. Then, looking at Cassie's face, he shouted, "Who cares about dumb old picnics, anyway?" He hopped on his bike and sped toward town.

"Danny, don't get too far ahead," Marc called. Turning to Cassie, he said, "You know you can get the day off."

"Maybe I don't want to," she snapped. Part of her knew she was being unfair, but another part of her couldn't forgive Danny. He had *promised* to take Sam in. And Marc—he just didn't understand. This afternoon he'd seemed so . . . so nice. She'd felt so close to him. Now, there seemed to be a wall between them, just like the wall between her and her mother and her and Danny. Suddenly, she felt terribly alone.

Marc shrugged and shook his head. "Okay," he said, "have it your way."

When they caught up to the bristly little figure waiting at the bottom of the hill, Marc said, "Hey, Danny, what did the man who gave you gum want?"

"Nothing much. He just wanted to know if I was Cassie's brother." And Danny jumped back on his bike and rode down Sail Street past the bay.

Chapter Fifteen

Cassie flopped on her bed, glad to be away from her mother and brother. Supper had been an ordeal—the kitchen lonely without Sam lying at her feet, Danny rattling on about the picnic, her mother promising she would ask for the day off. Then, while Danny and her mother waited silently at the kitchen table, Cassie had called Dr. Casey again.

Cassie had ignored Danny's breathless "How is he?" and had looked only at her mother, telling her, "Dr. Casey said that Sam is getting medication for his heart. They still don't know if he'll make it or not." Danny had slammed out the back door. Her mother had given her a quick hug, then gone in search of Danny.

She had called Liz, thinking she would understand. But all Liz could think of or talk about was the break-in at the Fairways' and how frightened she'd been. No one understands, Cassie thought. Mom says she does, but how can she? Sam has always been there for me. I don't remember ever not having him. Dad always said that as soon as he brought him home as a puppy, he was my dog. Why, he was part of our family before Danny. And he was part of our family when we were really a family—before Dad left us.

Outside, a warm breeze whispered through treetops but failed to lift the heavy, moist air. Images drifted through Cassie's mind. Sam, lying helpless; Mrs. Wentworth saying, 'They took my lavaliere, Cassie, my wedding gift from Hobart.'; Mr. O'Reilly, no longer interested in checkers; the two men talking in the woods; the dank, suffocating tunnel; Marc, frowning and distant; Danny, silent and sullen.

She could hear her mother moving around. Shutting windows, locking doors, climbing the stairs, opening the door to Danny's room, closing it. Cassie closed her eyes and turned on her side, hoping her mother wouldn't come in. Her door clicked open; her mother stepped in, hesitated, then left the room.

Cassie got up and went to the back window. Kneeling, she folded her arms on the sill, rested her head on them, and looked out into the deeper black of the woods where Sam had been poisoned. An insect droned by in the muggy air, then bumped against the screen.

Our family seems to be falling apart, she thought. Everything's going wrong. Mom is upset because I won't tell Danny I don't blame him about Sam. Maybe Danny is sorry—but he begged me to leave Sam out. How can I ever forgive him if Sam dies? "I wish Sam were here," she murmured. Her arms ached to reach out and feel the big collie's silken warmth.

And now Marc. He had begun to make the move to Kittiwake Bay tolerable. She had felt so close to him. He was easy to talk to, and they had fun together. And today, when he'd held her close . . . but tonight, when they had sat on the back step making plans, she had caught him studying her, his brows drawn together. He had seemed withdrawn, not his usual, smiling self.

Cassie thought about the emerald earring she'd found, now safely hidden in her small jewelry box. She would give it to the police eventually, but for now, she and Marc had decided to tell no one about their discoveries. Before they did, they wanted to find out who the third person was and where the items stolen from Waterview Manor were hidden. And what if they did tell the police about Sailor's plan for next week? Would they believe them? And, if they did believe them, would they search the tunnels and scare the thieves away? Then Mrs. Wentworth and Mr. O'Reilly would never get their treasures back. Besides, Sailor and Jake might change their plans and never show up. Then the police would think she and Marc had made up the whole story.

Cassie stood up and shook her left leg, numb from the knee down. Blood flowed back in, bringing prickles of pins and needles. She hobbled back to bed, then lay there staring at the shadowy ceiling, wishing for sleep. But thoughts kept whirling through her head, keeping her awake.

Chapter Sixteen

Finally, Wednesday arrived—oppressive, hot, and moist—threatening storms. For days, a scorching sun had blazed down, its intensity heightening the despondent mood prevalent at Waterview Manor. It was time for Cassie and Marc to put their plan into action.

Cassie, her heart hammering, opened the screen door and stepped into the quiet central hall of Waterview. Ryan, carrying a tray of dishes from the dining room, stopped short when he saw her. "What are you doing here?" he asked sharply.

"Just visiting Mrs. Wentworth and Mr. O'Reilly," Cassie answered, wide-eyed. "They've been feeling kind of down lately, what with the thefts and all."

Ryan muttered something that sounded like

"Goody Two-shoes," and stomped toward the kitchen.

Cassie found Mr. O'Reilly and Mr. Johnson on the porch, creaking back and forth in rockers and looking out at the bay. A sudden gust of wind set the unoccupied rockers into motion. "That wind smells of rain," said Mr. Johnson, wiping his brow with a large white handkerchief.

"That'd be nice. Cool things off," Mr. O'Reilly said. "Hi there, Cassie," he said as Cassie pulled a chair close to them. "Hot enough for you?"

"Too hot," Cassie said, lifting her ponytail from her neck. "Where's Mrs. Wentworth?"

"Some interview she wanted to catch on TV. She'll be out later and ask for that dratted Strauss music. Something different would be nice for a change."

Cassie smiled. "You're not fooling me, Mr. O'Reilly. I've seen you keeping time to the music." She settled into her chair and looked out over the bay. The fading sun glazed the sky an angry red. Cassie could hear the faraway crash of surf against the cliff, but the bay looked calm. She wondered how rain would affect the thieves' plans. She remembered the one called Sailor saying he had to sail with the tide. What would a storm do to the tide? Would they call the whole thing off?

"Hey, folks," Ryan called, coming through the game room door. "Mrs. Sawyer says a storm's coming, and not to stay out here too long."

"Did she now?" Mr. Johnson grumbled. "You tell her I'm an old sailor and I like to watch a stormy sea."

"Don't say I didn't warn you," Ryan said. Turning to Mr. O'Reilly, he asked, "How come you and Cassie aren't playing checkers tonight?"

"Just don't feel like it, Ryan," said Mr. O'Reilly, clicking his teeth together.

"Bet you're afraid she'll beat you," said Ryan, baiting him.

"Um. She might. She's got a good mind and a quick eye."

"How about a game, Mr. O'Reilly? It's been a long time now," Cassie asked.

"Well, all right. Bring out the set."

"I'll set it up for you in the game room," Ryan offered, hurrying across the wooden boards.

Cassie and Mr. O'Reilly followed him. At the door, Cassie called to Mr. Johnson, "Don't stay out here too long, Mr. Johnson. That wind might blow you away."

Mr. Johnson laughed and patted his round stomach. "Not much chance of that, Cassie."

In the game room, Cassie looked at Ryan to

thank him, but he slid his eyes away from hers and glanced at his watch. "Time for me to go. See you tomorrow," he said abruptly.

Mr. O'Reilly, watching Ryan walk away, said, "He's a strange one. Sometimes friendly. Sometimes not."

"I guess," said Cassie, distracted, her stomach tightening as she thought of Marc hiding outside, watching for a signal from the tower. With Ryan gone, it would be easier for her to slip out and check with Marc at their agreed-upon times.

"Well," said Mr. O'Reilly, "I suppose you young ones have your troubles, too."

Cassie nodded, thinking about Ryan. Liz really liked him. She said it wasn't just because he was "scrumptious," but because he seemed kind of lost. But Cassie didn't quite trust him. She wondered why he had urged her and Mr. O'Reilly to play checkers. Why hadn't he suggested Mr. Johnson play? He was sitting right there.

His sudden helpfulness made her suspicious. Earlier, he had seemed upset when she walked through the door. Doubt gnawed at her. Who was sending the signal from the tower? John Hudson had left a half hour ago, and now Ryan was leaving. Or were they? Was one of them, at this very minute, stealing up to the tower? Had Ryan wanted her to play checkers to keep her occupied?

Cassie looked at her watch—8:00 P.M. High tide was at 10:40. Marc had said that whoever navigated a boat through the cliff opening on the secret lake would have to do so just as the tide started to ebb.

"Cassie, you're not concentrating," said Mr. O'Reilly, jumping her last man.

Cassie glanced at her watch again. It was time to meet Marc and find out if he'd seen a signal. "I'm sorry, Mr. O'Reilly. My mind's just not on the game tonight. Why don't I get Mr. Johnson in out of the wind and you two can play?"

Cassie opened the door to the porch, and wind tore into the room. Mr. Johnson grumbled, but slowly heaved himself from his rocking chair and huffed his way into the game room.

"Back in a minute," said Cassie, hurrying into the dining room.

Cassie heard the whir of Mrs. Wentworth's wheelchair before she heard her voice. "Cassie! Cassie!" she called. "There you are, dear. Now I can hear my Strauss and visit with you."

Cassie hesitated. She didn't want to be rude, but it was time to meet Marc.

Mrs. Wentworth shook her head back and forth. "That Ryan! He dashed right by me. Wouldn't stop a minute to put the tape on."

Cassie relented and went to search for a Strauss tape. She smiled, thinking how Mrs. Wentworth sounded more like her old self.

"Thank you, Cassie," said the old woman, her hand automatically reaching for the lavaliere that no longer hung around her neck. "Now where are you off to?"

Impulsively, Cassie bent and kissed her satiny cheek. Maybe Mrs. Wentworth would have her treasured necklace back tomorrow. "I'll be right back. I promise."

Outside, Cassie slipped over to the boulder Marc had told her he would hide behind. No Marc! Where could he be? He was supposed to be watching for a signal from the tower! Cassie looked at her watch—8:15. Ryan had left a while ago. Had he gone to the tower? He'd had just about enough time by now. Or had Ryan really left and was John Hudson lumbering up the rickety stairs to the lookout?

Heavy clouds scudded across the darkening sky, and the increasing wind blew through the low-growing trees. Cassie looked up at the looming tower. She felt the muscles in her neck and shoulders tighten as the minutes ticked slowly by. She should go back in. Mrs. Wentworth would wonder what happened to her. Then, high in the tower window, a light flashed three times. Stopped. Then again flashed three times. Jake would be starting through the tunnel above Sail Street, and whoever was in the tower would be sneaking to the cellar.

Whoever was in the tower . . . It must be Ryan. Oh, where was Marc? He was supposed to follow the thief to the cellar while she called the police. Should she call the police, anyway? What could she tell them? Would they believe her?

As she stood on the desolate cliff high above the thrashing Atlantic, a high-pitched moaning wind was her only answer. Quickly, she decided: She would go to the cellar alone. They were too close to solving the mystery to let it slip away. Then, if someone did meet Jake at the tunnel entrance, she would rush back and call the police.

Cassie hurried in and, after telling Mrs. Wentworth, Mr. O'Reilly, and Mr. Johnson that she was leaving because she wanted to get home before the storm broke, went back to the central hall. Except for the strains of a Strauss waltz, the old mansion was still, the other residents already retired to their rooms.

A blast of wind rattled the doors and windows in their casements. Blood pounding in her ears,

Cassie picked up a flashlight she had secreted behind a sofa pillow and stole into the shadowy dimness of the east wing.

In the vestibule at the far east end, wind howled its eerie scream through the cracked windows. The basement door was closed. Had the person in the tower had time to get here? Cassie pressed her ear against the wood panel—the creak of a footstep on the stairs? She waited. Silence. Cautiously, she opened the door.

She stepped onto the first of the steep stairs and, stomach knotting, closed the heavy door behind her. Blackness enveloped her. Damp, fetid air filled her nostrils. The thought of those squirming beetles overhead made her skin crawl.

She waited for her eyes to adjust to the darkness. It was slightly lighter near the ceiling to the front, where small slits of windows rattled from clouts of wind. She crept slowly down the stairs, pressing her heel against the back of each step. In the distance, she saw a feebly probing light, and in an instant realized it must be the intruder.

Cassie didn't dare snap on her own light. Gradually, she was able to discern the darker bulk of discarded furniture. Stealthily, she stole from object to object in the cluttered basement, careful to stay behind large pieces, careful not to bump into anything. She concentrated on following the dim, bobbing light, willing herself not to think of the creepy things swarming in the wooden beams above her head.

Her foot hit something and sent it skittering softly across the floor. The figure in front of her turned and swept his light swiftly around. Cassie, her heart threatening to burst through her chest, shrank back behind a large bookcase.

The figure waited a moment, then continued his journey down the cavernous black cellar. The shadow of a discarded rocking horse galloped ahead of his moving circle of light. He turned to the right, then, kneeling, propped his flashlight on the floor, illuminating a large trunk. Cassie, flattened against an old chest of drawers, heard the clicking of a lock. She studied the figure in the shadowy light. He was Ryan's size and build, not John's. He swept his hand through his hair.

Marc! Marc always does that. No! No! Not Marc!

She squinted, concentrating on the dark figure. Marc and Ryan are about the same size, she thought. It can't be Marc! He's my friend. Every nerve in her body stretched to breaking point. Where was Marc tonight? Why hadn't he been outside?

Jumbled thoughts flew through her mind. Marc

knew a lot about boats and tides. Marc had disappeared up Waterview Way that first night. Marc could have known about the tunnels before and pretended not to. Marc had followed her to the tower. Marc knew that she was afraid of tunnels, that she would never go in one again.

Tears stung her eyes. It can't be Marc!

The trunk lid groaned open. The silent figure reached in, picked up a package, closed the trunk, picked up his light, and continued on down the cellar. He walked straight to the massive chest that concealed the trapdoor, stepped behind it, and pulled up the heavy lid.

Cassie, moving nearer, could hear a muffled voice float up from the tunnel. "About time. Let's move it. Everything's going wrong, and it's almost high tide. Sailor's got to get out of here with this stuff tonight."

"Everything's here," said the other person. "I'll bring it down. Everything out of the tunnel room in the woods?"

"Yeah. Everything's out of there, but we've got a new problem."

"What do you mean?"

Cassie inched closer. She had to know who the third thief was. Their voices rose from the blackness below.

"You know that snoopy redheaded girl, the one with the dog, or the one that used to have the dog." The man laughed evilly.

Cassie recognized Jake's voice. A surge of anger shot through her. It was because of that wicked man Sam was still lying in the hospital.

"I know. I know. I still don't see why you had to poison her dog. He would never have led anyone to the tunnel."

"Don't be so sure of that. Tonight guess who I find snooping around there?" said Jake. Without waiting for an answer, he added, "Her brother. Snooping must run in the family."

Cassie's heart stopped. Danny! What was Danny doing there, and what had Jake done to him?

"You mean Danny Hartt? What did you do with him?" asked the other voice sharply.

"What could I do?" whined Jake. "I couldn't very well leave him there to tell everyone about the tunnel, could I? I caught sight of him just as I started climbing down. Standing there watching me, dumbfounded. Boy, I sure moved fast. Caught him in no time. But look what the brat did to me. Scratched me up something fierce."

"Where is he now?" asked the other voice.

It's Ryan, thought Cassie, listening intently. It's Ryan, not Marc. Relief flooded through her. Then fear stabbed at her again. She knew Marc would never hurt Danny, but what about Ryan?

"Don't get so excited," said Jake. "He's right here. We'll take him to Sailor and let him decide what to do with him."

"You brought him with you?" asked Ryan incredulously. "That wasn't smart."

A hand reached up and clanged the iron door closed. The harsh sound hit Cassie's center like a physical blow. Danny. Her little brother. She had to save him!

Chapter Seventeen

Cassie stood frozen in the darkness. Her head reeled, and her heart pounded in her throat. Every inch of her body wanted to flee, to run back through the tomblike cellar, through the lifeless labyrinth of hallways, to the center hall where she could get help, where she could call the police. But was there time? If she did that, would the police get there in time to help Danny? And if they didn't, what would happen to him?

Cassie took one last look toward her escape route through the dark cellar, then forced her legs to bend and knelt. She pressed her ear against the trapdoor and listened until she could no longer hear movement or voices from below. Cautiously, she pulled the heavy door open. She stared into the black pit below her. A wave of claustrophobia clutched at her throat. She couldn't breathe. She couldn't move.

She'd sworn she'd never go in a tunnel again. But Danny was in there, and she couldn't chance going for help. Saving Danny was up to her. How, she didn't know. But she knew she had to try.

Cassie stepped onto the first stone stair. Her mouth was dry. Her stomach churned. Cold chills shivered down her spine. Her heart palpitated furiously. She heard her own rapid, shallow breathing and knew she was hyperventilating. I can go in this tunnel, she told herself. There's plenty of air in there. This is all in my head. Suddenly she felt dizzy.

Cassie sat on the steps and cupped her hands over her nose and mouth—breathed in and out, in and out. Gradually the dizziness passed. Her breathing became more normal.

She tiptoed into the tunnel, placing each foot carefully to make sure she didn't send a loose stone scuttling. A web, strong and sticky, clung to her nose and mouth. Panic rose. She clawed the web from her face, her nails scratching her own flesh.

The image of the trapped fish struggling for breath flashed before her. Would she be trapped by Sailor, Jake, and Ryan? No! Somehow, she would get Danny out of there.

Willing herself to calm down, she stood in the darkness, not daring to turn on her light. Every nerve in her body tingling, she waited to get her bearings.

With outstretched hands lightly touching either wall, she groped her way along the tunnel leading to the secret lake. Rounding a curve, she saw a dim light fading into the distance and heard a muffled curse. She shrank back against the wall.

She waited until the sounds ahead of her faded, then inched forward. At the crawlway, another panic attack wracked her body. Waves of nausea swept over her. Her knees buckled, and her breathing quickened. Again, she pressed her hand against her mouth and breathed through her nose, waiting for the dizziness to subside.

Shaking off the thought of the cricket that had stuck to her palm, dead in its moldy shroud, she fell to her hands and knees. Shivering, she crept through the low crawlway. Finally, fresh air flowed against her face, and she smelled the salty sea. A thunderous rumbling echoed through the tunnel. Terrified, Cassie wondered if the tunnel was caving in.

As she turned the last curve, lightning split the sky and outlined the group before her. She hid behind a tall rock, scanning the cave for Danny. The men were quarreling. Their angry voices rose and fell, their words sometimes lost in a clap of thunder.

"I don't know why you brought him here, Jake," said Sailor. "Now he can identify us."

"I couldn't very well leave him there," growled Jake.

Sailor shouted, "Light those lanterns. Then let's get the boat loaded and ready to go. I've got to get out on the tide, and that storm's threatening to break. I'll decide later what to do with the kid."

Jake lit some lanterns and placed them in various spots, all the while snapping his gum. "Why don't you take him with you? Hold him for ransom," he suggested.

"I would," Sailor said irritably, "but there's no room in the boat. You know that. You keep him hidden till I contact you."

"I'm not hanging around this town," Jake argued. "I'm leaving tonight and meeting you tomorrow, just like we planned."

"Okay. Okay," Sailor snapped. "Bring the kid with you."

Ryan, his face frightening in a flicker of lightning, his voice tight with fear, said, "You never should have gotten me into this, Sailor. We're in big trouble now."

"You'll be glad enough when you get your share

of the cut, little brother," said Sailor. "Now pile that stuff you brought down in the runabout. Then help us with the rest of the loot."

Little brother? The words echoed in Cassie's mind, answering an unformed question.

She felt as if she were in a nightmare as she watched the three figures carrying boxes from the shadowy cave to the runabout that rested on the slope of the entrance. Sailor picked up a lantern and went to check the smaller cave, where Cassie had found the emerald earring.

A flash of lightning illuminated the great perpendicular walls of granite that encircled the secret lake. Finally, Cassie spied Danny, a pale shadow in the darker shadow of rocks, not more than twenty feet from her.

It would take no time to reach him. But if she stepped forward, she would be in a circle of light falling from a lantern. She considered tossing small stones at Danny, but was afraid he'd call out and alert the others.

Another flare of lightning. Thunder boomed, and the wind shrieked. Cassie saw Danny clap his hands over his ears and shrink farther back among the rocks.

"I'd better hurry and get out of here," Sailor shouted. "I'll see you tomorrow as planned. We'll decide then what to do with the kid. Now give me a hand with this boat."

The three men bent and pushed the boat toward the lake. Cassie knew this was the chance she'd been waiting for. She'd only have a minute before Jake and Ryan started back. She rushed to Danny, grabbed his hand, and hustled him into the dark cover of the tunnel.

Jake shouted, "Hey. Where did the kid go?"

Ryan's voice rose in an answering shout: "Don't worry about him. He can't get very far. And he could never open that trapdoor. I'll go after him while you help Sailor launch the boat."

Cassie heard enough to know that Ryan was following them, then their voices faded and were lost in a peal of thunder.

"Come on, Danny," she whispered to her trembling brother. "Follow me."

Guided by her sharpened senses, Cassie raced toward the crawlway. Her breathing was deep and steady. She pushed Danny into the opening before her, urging him to hurry. No waves of claustrophobia washed over her. All of her energy was concentrated on getting away. They scrambled through the narrow opening, stood up, and ran as quickly as space and light allowed.

Soon, Ryan's voice echoed through the tunnel:

"Danny, wait. I won't hurt you. Wait for me."

"Come on, Danny," Cassie urged. "We're almost there."

What would Ryan do if he caught them? She didn't know. She couldn't be sure. But Jake would be right behind him, and . . . if only they could get to the cellar first. She could slam the trapdoor shut and push that chest over it. Then no one could follow them.

Danny slipped and cried out in pain. Cassie helped him up. Ryan's pounding feet thundered closer. Finally, her light picked out the stone steps. She pushed Danny ahead of her and started after him.

Ryan's light discovered her, and she heard Jake yell, "Grab her. Don't let her get away."

Cassie stumbled up the stone steps. She was nearly through the opening when Ryan grabbed her ankle. With a fierce jerk, she pulled her foot loose, jumped up, and slammed the trapdoor shut. "Danny, sit on this door," she shouted, pushing at the heavy chest.

Danny sat on the door, which started to lift against his slight weight. Cassie heard scuffling sounds from below. Adrenaline rushed through her veins. She shoved with all her strength, and the heavy chest slid over the door.

Trembling with relief, she took Danny in her arms. Tears slid from beneath her closed eyes.

"You're not mad at me anymore, Cassie?" asked Danny, his voice muffled against her shoulder.

"Oh, Danny. No, I'm not mad anymore. Come on. We have to get out of here and call the police."

Danny held back. "But, Cassie, I did it on purpose," he sobbed.

"Danny, we have to get out of here," Cassie urged.

Danny wouldn't move. Words poured from him. "I was mad at you, Cassie. You've got new friends and you didn't want me around. Mommy's never home . . . and Tommy keeps calling me 'Fire Head.' You were so bossy. So I let Sam stay out. But, Cassie, I never thought he'd get hurt . . . it's all my fault . . . and now Sam's going to die. . . ." Danny's confession ended in a torrent of tears.

Guilt rushed through Cassie. She'd been so preoccupied with herself that summer, she hadn't realized how Danny felt. She pulled him close and hugged him hard. "I'm sorry, too, Danny. But everything's going to be all right."

Something thudded against the trapdoor, making it quiver. Cassie grabbed Danny's hand and half dragged him up the sloping floor toward the exit at the east wing. They can't open that door, she thought. But every so often, she glanced over her shoulder. She didn't want to be trapped in this black pit with Jake and Ryan.

At last they were clambering up the stairs to the vestibule. As she flung the door open, acrid smoke drifted in. Fire! Cassie thought, panic clutching at her stomach. We can't go back in the cellar. These windows are all boarded up. We're trapped!

She flashed her light around the enclosure. Smoke curled under the door leading to the front of the house. By now, tears stung Cassie's eyes, and her choking cough was echoed by Danny's.

"We'll go the back way, Danny," she gasped.

Danny clung to Cassie. "My leg hurts," he moaned.

"We've got to get out of here, Danny! Get down low. It's easier to breathe near the floor. Scoot along behind me."

"My leg," Danny sobbed.

"I'll check it in a minute, Danny. We've got to get out of here! Now!"

Cassie opened the back door of the vestibule, pushed Danny through, then slammed the door shut. Here, the smoke wasn't as heavy. She focused her light on Danny's leg. Blood flowed from a nasty cut on his right knee. Deftly, Cassie tore off a sneaker and sock, then secured the white sock around Danny's knee.

"That should stop the bleeding. Later, we'll have a doctor look at it."

They climbed the stairs to the back of the house. Frantically, Cassie searched for the flight that led to the balcony high above the cliff. They stumbled up the steep steps. The door creaked and groaned like a live animal. When Cassie turned the knob, the door banged against her, and moisture-laden wind swept in, plastering their clothes against them.

They struggled out onto the balcony, and Cassie pulled the door tight behind them. The fire ladder would lead them to safety. Cassie gasped as the balcony swayed in the bellowing wind. Lightning split the blue-black sky. With horror, Cassie watched the ladder rip away from the balcony to crash on jagged rocks far below. "Stay close to the house, away from the railing," she shouted. "There's another way out of here."

With a roar, the dark sky blazed with light. Flames burst through the roof of the east wing. "Cassie, I'm scared," sobbed Danny, squeezing her hand so tightly, her ring bit into her skin.

So am I, thought Cassie. So am I.

"We can make it, Danny. But we have to get to

the big porch. And we have to get there before the fire does."

Flames crackled. The ocean crashed and bellowed. Cassie's mouth was dry. Her ears roared with the fury of the wind, fire, and her own racing blood. She clung to Danny's hand as fiercely as he clung to hers.

A wrenching sound tore the air. Looking back, Cassie saw, as though in slow motion, part of the balcony fall away from the house and fly out over the cliff.

"Don't look back, Danny," she screamed. "We're almost there."

Cassie fumbled with the door to the back hallway. Inside, swirling wreaths of smoke choked them. They clattered down the stairs and out onto the veranda. Panting, they staggered through the dining room to the center hall.

Here everything was in confusion. Some firemen played hoses of water on the burning east wing; others carried elderly residents from the west wing.

Outside, in the brilliant glow from the lightning, fire, and rotating signals on police cars, the residents stood with Mrs. Sawyer, watching their home burn down. Kittiwake's one ambulance screeched up Waterview Way.

Cassie, with Danny limping beside her, walked out into the confusion.

"Look. There's Cassie," shouted John Hudson.

Marc left a police officer he was talking to and ran to Cassie. "Thank God you're all right," he said, putting his arms around her and holding her close. "They've caught Ryan and that guy Jake. I couldn't believe it when Ryan said you and Danny were in the tunnel! Then the fire started. I was crazy worried about you."

Cassie, weak with the relief of safety, leaned against him. "Where were you, Marc?" she asked.

"I got mugged," he said, laughing ruefully.

"What happened?" she cried, noticing the bloody lump on his forehead.

Marc gingerly put his hand to the lump. "I was watching for the signal when someone sneaked up behind me and clobbered me. I found out later it was Ryan. I got this bump when I fell on some rocks. I don't know how long I was out." He nodded toward John. "John found me. He was bringing ice cream back for Mr. Johnson and he heard me moaning."

Cassie looked at John, who stood nearby, a proud grin lighting his heavy features.

The police lieutenant Marc had been talking to walked over. "Is this the young lady you've been telling me about?" he asked.

"Yes, Lieutenant," answered Marc. "This is Cassie."

"Glad to see you and your brother safe and sound, Cassie. I'll let my men know. They've been searching for you. You and your boyfriend wait for me over there with the others. I want to talk to you."

"My brother's cut his leg," said Cassie, pulling Danny close.

"We'll have a paramedic take a look at it," Lieutenant Watson promised.

"The fire?" Cassie said. "Did the thieves start it?"

The lieutenant shook his head. "We don't know for sure. But it was probably lightning. The experts will find out."

Cassie, Marc, and Danny walked over to the elderly people. The blazing fire illuminated their stricken faces as they watched firemen hose the burning mansion. Paramedics moved among them, giving first aid and helping them to the ambulance. Lightning flashed and thunder boomed, but still no rain fell.

"Cassie! Look! Here's Cassie! Thank God you're safe, dear!" said Mrs. Wentworth from her wheelchair. A tremulous smile lifted the corners of her mouth, and tears streamed down her parchmentlike cheeks.

Cassie let the tears fall as she was engulfed in bear hugs from Mr. Johnson, Mr. O'Reilly, and the other old folks. Wiping her face with her hands, she watched John tenderly assist Mrs. Wentworth from her wheelchair onto an ambulance cot. She flushed with shame, remembering her suspicions of him.

The ambulance left with its first load of passengers. No one had suffered burns, but some people were in shock.

As Cassie started back to Danny, she heard the motor of a nearby police car start. As the engine revved up, Ryan called to her. She froze to the spot, then turned to look at him. "Cassie!" he shouted, "I want you to know I had nothing to do with poisoning your dog, and I would never have let you or Danny get hurt."

Jake, handcuffed to him, gave a disgusted grunt, and turned to look out the other window.

Cassie stared at Ryan but said nothing. She wanted to believe him but knew she could never be sure.

"Cassie," Ryan pleaded, "believe me. It all started with my brother and me looking for treasure. I never expected to get involved in stealing, but my brother . . . he . . . can't you understand, Cassie? He's my brother, and I wanted him to . . ."

The car drove away, and Cassie could no longer hear Ryan, but she could see the pale oval of his face and the darkness of his eyes as he looked back at her.

"Cassie," Lieutenant Watson called, striding over to her, "I thought you'd like to know that my men just picked up Mike Jerrick. He was headed down the coast. They got him and all the stolen goods in his boat."

"How did you know what was going on?" asked Cassie, trying to piece things together.

"Your boyfriend there," said the lieutenant, nodding toward Marc. "He called us. And your mother called to report your brother missing. We've sent a car for her, and she'll meet you at the hospital. Come on," he said, turning to Danny, "the ambulance is back for you, young man."

Lieutenant Watson picked up Danny and carried him to the waiting ambulance. Cassie and Marc followed and climbed in beside him. Cassie sat on the edge of Danny's cot and reached for his hand. She heard a great sigh escape Marc as he sat down on the other cot. Tears of exhaustion streamed silently down her cheeks. The ambulance, lights flashing, started down Waterview Way.

Looking out the back window, Cassie watched, as though in a dream, the firemen spraying the towering mansion. She saw flames leap from the east wing to the tower. Then, at last, clouds opened and rain fell in sweeping, gusty sheets.

Chapter Eighteen

Mrs. Wentworth's eyes sparkled, and her frail hand lovingly fingered the lavaliere that lay against her chest. "You two have certainly added to my list of stories to tell," she said to Cassie and Marc.

Lieutenant Watson had driven Cassie and Marc to Kittiwake Hospital. They had spent the morning with him at the police station, telling him everything they knew about the robberies and tunnels, and Cassie had given him the emerald earring. Now they were returning Mrs. Wentworth's lavaliere and Mr. O'Reilly's chess set to them.

The four of them were in the green-and-white-striped visitors' lounge. The residents from Waterview Manor had been admitted to the hospital and treated as necessary. No one had been seriously injured, and most of them, including Mrs. Wentworth and Mr. O'Reilly, would soon leave to stay with relatives or friends. A few would be transferred to nursing homes in neighboring towns.

"Well, Patrick O'Reilly, you seem pleased to have that chess set of yours back," Mrs. Wentworth said, cocking her head to the side.

Mr. O'Reilly was placing his chess pieces on a table, caressing each piece. He grinned at Mrs. Wentworth. "Yep, Isabelle, I've got my chess set back. Thanks to Cassie there," he said, his dentures clicking.

"You were right about one thing, Mrs. Wentworth," Marc said. "The tunnel does lead to the ocean, not the bay."

"Hmph. I'm right about more than one thing, young man," Mrs. Wentworth quipped.

"I'm going to miss you two," Cassie said in an unsteady voice.

"Nonsense, miss," Mrs. Wentworth said sharply. "No tears now. Before you know it, Waterview Manor will be rebuilt and we'll be back there." She paused and fingered her lavaliere. In a softer tone, she murmured, "Of course, it won't be the same . . ."

"Don't go getting sentimental, Isabelle," Mr.

O'Reilly said. "It will be a whole lot better and a darn sight safer."

When she said good-bye, Cassie bent and planted a kiss on Mrs. Wentworth's wrinkled cheek, then on Mr. O'Reilly's.

Jean Hartt handed Cassie a bowl of freshly popped popcorn, and Cassie drizzled melted butter over it. Mrs. Hartt squeezed Cassie's shoulders. "I'm so proud of you, Cass. Going in that tunnel for Danny, and hating close spaces like you do. But, please—no more adventures! Just a nice steady routine for what's left of the summer."

Cassie grinned and said, "But no one's found Captain Kidd's treasure yet."

"Never mind Captain Kidd's treasure. There's been enough excitement in this house to last us a lifetime."

Cassie turned and hugged her mother. "I agree," she murmured.

Mrs. Hartt dabbed at her eyes with a napkin, then opened the refrigerator door. "You bring in the popcorn, Cass, and I'll get the soda."

Cassie set the bowl on the low table in front of the living-room couch. Liz, shifting Minerva on her lap, reached for a handful.

Cassie sat on the floor, her back against a chair,

her right hand stroking Sam's silky head. Her mother had helped her bring him home that afternoon.

"What did you do then?" Liz asked Marc, tossing popcorn, piece by piece, into her mouth.

Marc scooted down from a chair and settled in front of the table. "When Mrs. Wentworth told me Cassie had left, I knew she must have seen the signal and followed the thief herself. And I figured whoever had given that signal was the person who had hit me."

"Weren't you afraid, Cassie, to go in that cellar by yourself?" Liz asked, her voice full of admiration.

Marc laughed and scooped up a handful of popcorn. "Never mind the cellar. I didn't think she'd ever go in a tunnel again. But somehow . . . she did it."

Cassie shuddered, remembering.

"Danny was in there," Liz said softly. "That's why. And then the fire. You and Danny must have been petrified, Cassie!" Liz stopped eating. A frown creased her brow. "The fire. I wonder if Ryan—"

"No," Marc said. "Lieutenant Watson told us the fire chief confirmed lightning started the fire. It seems it traveled along an electrical wire, then smoldered in those old wooden walls awhile before it burst through."

Cassie looked down to hide the quick tears that sprang to her eyes, remembering the rickety balcony and Danny clutching her hand. Now she wondered how they had ever made it. But they were safe, and so was Sam, she thought, digging her hand in the ruff of silken hair around his neck.

"How did Danny end up there, anyway? How did he even know about the tunnel?" Liz wondered.

"He overheard Cassie and me talking," Marc explained. "Then he decided to help us."

"He eavesdropped," Cassie said, smiling. "He was hiding behind the bushes while Marc and I sat on the back step making plans."

Marc nodded and, looking at Cassie, said quietly, "He felt pretty bad."

"About what?" Liz asked.

"About Sam," Cassie said. "He was supposed to take Sam in the night he got into the poisoned meat."

Sam opened his eyes and thumped his tail. He looked at Minerva, yawned, and settled himself more comfortably.

"Then Jake found him," Marc said.

"I really don't think Ryan would have hurt

Danny," Cassie murmured, thinking of Ryan's words that night. "I guess he got involved because of his brother. At first, they were only looking for treasure, or so his brother told him."

Marc finished his soda. "That must be why Ryan said Mrs. Wentworth went loony. He didn't want anyone else to believe her stories and go searching for the tunnel."

Liz, fiddling with her tiny braid, gazed out the window. "I guess I'm the loony one—believing Ryan. That camera he gave me to use? It was stolen. I turned it over to the police."

Cassie said softly, "You aren't loony, Liz."

"My dad said Ryan used to worship his older brother. He always followed him around town, like a shadow. I'd forgotten about the trouble Mike got into years ago. I was just a little kid then."

"What kind of trouble?" Cassie asked.

"He was great with boats and always won the annual sailboat race. My dad said that's why he was nicknamed 'Sailor.' I guess people bet on the race, and he was the favorite to win. Then, one year he lost and no one could understand why. They found out later he had lost on purpose, so he could make a lot of money on the bets. My dad said he left town after that, and hadn't come back in all these years. There were rumors, though, that he'd been getting into trouble."

"That would explain why Sailor, or Mike, sounded bitter every time he mentioned Kittiwake Bay," Cassie said. "But didn't Ryan ever talk about him?"

"Not to me," Marc said.

"Hardly ever," Liz said, settling Minerva more comfortably. Looking at Marc, she asked, "What happened after you found out Cassie wasn't in Waterview?"

"I called the police and told them everything we'd found out—about the tunnels and the stolen goods, and how Cassie was missing. At first, Lieutenant Watson didn't seem to believe me, but when I told him about the earring Cassie had found, he sounded more interested. Later, they caught Ryan and Jake on the cliff above the bay."

"How come that guy, Jake, poisoned Sam?" Liz asked.

Cassie's arm tightened about Sam, who again thumped his tail. "He didn't want Sam nosing around in the woods. He thought I might follow him, and Jake and Ryan used the woods as a cover to get to the tunnel with stolen goods."

"I want to see all these tunnels," Liz said. She was silent for a moment. Then, looking from Marc to Cassie, she said slowly, "It must have been Jake who robbed the Fairways while Ryan kept me on the phone."

Cassie returned Liz's gaze, her own eyes dark with sympathy. She knew how much Liz had liked Ryan and how his betrayal must hurt.

Marc, breaking the silence, asked, "Who's going to the Labor Day picnic Saturday—Kittiwake's big bash?"

Cassie looked up at Danny, who had just limped into the room, a large bandage encircling his right knee. "We wouldn't miss it, would we, Danny?"

"We sure wouldn't," Danny said. "Mom, Cassie, and me are going. Hey! The popcorn's all gone," he yelled.

"Danny," Liz said, leaning forward. "Guess what! Minerva's going to have kittens."

Danny dashed toward the kitchen and collided with his mother, who was coming into the living room. "Mom! Minerva's going to have kittens. Can I have one? Can I?"

Danny's eyes were round, and his fiery hair seemed to stand on end. Cassie smiled as their mother ruffled his head.

"I guess we could add a kitten to our household. They're pretty little, and Sam seems to have accepted Minerva as a visitor. Listen, you two," she said, looking from Danny to Cassie. "I have to go to work now, and I want you to stay right here at home, okay?"

"Okay," Cassie said.

Sighing, Mrs. Hartt said, "I wish I didn't have to work these late hours. . . . Now where did I put my keys?"

Cassie gave Sam a quick hug before getting to her feet. She walked over to the television set and picked up the keys.

"Thanks, Cass," Mrs. Hartt said. She bent to kiss Danny good-bye, but he squirmed away and wiped his cheek. "See you all later," she called, hurrying out the door.

"I'll make some more popcorn," Cassie offered.

"I'll help," Marc said, getting to his feet.

As Cassie waited for him in the doorway, she looked back at her brother and Liz. Danny had flopped down next to Liz and was stroking Minerva, who purred like a motorboat. "When will the kittens be born, Liz?" she heard him ask.

Sam raised his head, yawned, then tucked his long snout between his outstretched paws and closed his eyes. A rush of happiness swept through Cassie. Kittiwake Bay was home now.

Marc followed her to the kitchen. He was close by her side when she reached for the jar of popcorn. His nearness brought a flush to her face, and her heartbeat quickened. He's taller than I am now, she thought; he must have grown some this summer.

Marc took her by the shoulders and turned her toward him. "You've got at least ten freckles," he said, lightly touching the tip of her nose.

"They're seasonal," Cassie said. "I get them every summer. But your hair is always in your eyes." And she reached up to brush it back before he kissed her.

Dear Reader,

I've always enjoyed spine-tingling mysteries. In writing this book, I combined my love of mysteries with my love of the Maine coast, where the high cliffs and surging waters make an exciting and dangerous setting for Cassie Hartt's adventures.

I hope you enjoyed your journey with Cassie and her friends!

Joyce A. Stengel